DR. MORELLE TAKES A BOW

Miss Frayle, no longer employed by psychiatrist and detective Dr. Morelle, now works as secretary to Hugo Coltman, head of a drama school. Endeavouring to entice her back, Dr. Morelle accepts an invitation to lecture at the school, only to become entangled in the sinister schemes that threaten the lives of students and teachers. After a brutal murder, tension mounts as Dr. Morelle and Miss Frayle find themselves targeted by the killer. Can Dr. Morelle's investigation be successfully concluded, and the murderer unmasked?

Books by Ernest Dudley
in the Linford Mystery Library:

ALIBI AND DR. MORELLE
THE HARASSED HERO
CONFESS TO DR. MORELLE
THE MIND OF DR. MORELLE
DR. MORELLE AND DESTINY
CALLERS FOR DR. MORELLE
LOOK OUT FOR LUCIFER!
MENACE FOR DR. MORELLE
NIGHTMARE FOR DR. MORELLE
THE WHISTLING SANDS
TO LOVE AND PERISH

ERNEST DUDLEY

DR. MORELLE TAKES A BOW

Complete and Unabridged

LINFORD
Leicester

First published in Great Britain

First Linford Edition
published 2007

British Library CIP Data

Dudley, Ernest
    Dr. Morelle takes a bow.—Large print ed.—
Linford mystery library
1. Morelle, Doctor (Fictitious character)—
Fiction 2. Detective and mystery stories
3. Large type books
I. Title
823.9'14 [F]

ISBN 978–1–84617–675–3

Published by
F. A. Thorpe (Publishing)
Anstey, Leicestershire

Set by Words & Graphics Ltd.
Anstey, Leicestershire
Printed and bound in Great Britain by
T. J. International Ltd., Padstow, Cornwall

This book is printed on acid-free paper

1

Miss Frayle sat down at the end of one of the curving rows of seats and searched her mind for the reason behind the feeling of apprehension which agitated her. Her horn-rimmed glasses slid down her nose and she fumbled to push them back.

What could go wrong? Dr. Morelle had arrived. The hundred or so students were settling down.

Miss Frayle looked around the theatre. It was fashioned solidly, in a circular shape, and attached to the rambling bulk of the old mansion. There was an ornate dome, embellished with cupids and nymphs, and below the dome a series of high windows ran right round the building. A steep stairway at the back led up to an outside balustraded balcony upon which the windows opened.

Adapted skilfully by Hugo Coltman, the building, with its crimson drapes on the white-panelled walls, alternating with splendid oil paintings of Coltman in his greatest rôles, provided a useful theatre, fully equipped, for the plays and lectures which filled the students' days. Famous dramatic critics, producers and talent-scouts came regularly to see Coltman's pupils, and during the past few years many a young beginner had been discovered at this very theatre.

Miss Frayle glanced round. Jeff Sullivan, the fencing master, was sharing a joke with young, brooding Roy Allen, the singing teacher. And there was Elspeth Finch, the mime teacher, speaking sharply to a fair-haired girl student.

Miss Frayle sighed to herself. That acid tongue of Elspeth's made her so unpopular with everybody. Miss Frayle watched, as with a last vicious whisper, Elspeth Finch turned away from the girl and hovered near Roy Allen. Again Miss Frayle gave a tiny sigh. Elspeth was several years older than Allen; besides he gave her no encouragement.

Theodore Willard, diction and elocution, had now joined Sullivan and Allen, and then Miss Frayle's attention was distracted by a shower of flower-petals drifting down from one of the several large bowls of flowers which somebody had placed on the narrow ledge running inside the window.

Miss Frayle was idly wondering if the flowers had been disturbed by someone up there and who it could be when the stage curtains swished back dramatically. Hugo Coltman made his entrance from the wings followed by the familiar, gaunt figure of Dr. Morelle.

In his well-cut double-breasted suit, which did not quite succeed in disguising a comfortable paunch, the founder of the Coltman Drama Workshop held his fine head, with its mane of greying hair, haughtily. There was a quizzical expression in his slightly protuberant brown eyes. He motioned Dr. Morelle to a chair.

'It is a privilege and a pleasure,' he said, his rich baritone voice reaching effortlessly to the back of the theatre, 'to welcome Dr. Morelle. I am certain I can assure him on your behalf of the enthusiasm that has greeted his acceptance of my invitation to come and speak to us.'

So Hugo Coltman got into his stride, listening to and enjoying the sound of his voice. While the rich tones continued in his ear, Dr. Morelle's thoughts wandered.

He was careful not to allow his glance to stray in Miss Frayle's direction. While he would have smiled sardonically at the suggestion that Miss Frayle had been in any way necessary to him, yet the fact remained that ever since she had left him nothing seemed to have gone quite right at No. 221b Harley Street.

Take his most recent secretary, Miss Grimshaw, for instance. A pleasant young woman, shorthand impeccable, her typewriting more than competent. Nevertheless, Dr. Morelle had found her as disappointing as any of the others. And two nights ago Miss Grimshaw had left.

'If you imagine I'm going to work all hours of the night, every night of the week,' she had said, 'you've got another think coming, Dr. Morelle. Look at the

4

time. Twenty past ten, and I've been here since nine o'clock this morning.'

'In point of fact,' he had reminded her, 'you were five minutes late.'

'You're not human, that's your trouble,' Miss Grimshaw had said. 'You're a machine, and you expect other people to be the same. I'm not made of clockwork, so good night, Dr. Morelle, and good-bye.'

The study door had slammed loudly behind her while Dr. Morelle lit a Le Sphinx. Sombrely he began to turn over the mass of papers on his desk. As he unearthed the batch of notes he was seeking, the front-door bell rang.

Miss Grimshaw returning, he reflected. Either to ask for her salary, which, in the excitement of her departure, she had forgotten, or to offer her apologies and ask to be taken back.

If it were the latter, he was deciding, he would under the circumstances accede graciously to her request. He did not look up as the study door opened.

'Yes, Miss Grimshaw?' he said silkily, over his shoulder.

'Hello, Dr. Morelle.'

He had started up. This was the last person he had expected.

'Miss Frayle.' Quickly he recovered his poise. 'I was expecting Miss Grimshaw, returning to finish her work.'

'I'm so glad,' Miss Frayle said, 'that you've found someone else who doesn't mind working late hours.'

Dr. Morelle winced, opened his mouth to make an acid reply, but let it go. There was something quite nostalgic about Miss Frayle's gift for saying the wrong thing so soon after her arrival.

Miss Frayle had sat down, glancing round the familiar study. She explained how she had absent-mindedly retained the key to the front door when she left, and had been about to ring the bell when she remembered the key and decided to give Dr. Morelle a surprise.

'I was under the impression,' Dr. Morelle said, 'that you were happily employed at the dramatic academy — '

'Drama Workshop, Dr. Morelle,' Miss Frayle said. 'That's what Mr. Coltman likes it to be called.'

Dr. Morelle leaned forward slightly. 'Do I owe the unexpected pleasure of your visit to the fact that you have given up your post?'

'Oh, no,' Miss Frayle said. 'Besides, I am sure your — Miss Grimshaw, did you say her name was? — I am sure she's taking good care of you. As a matter of fact, I've come on behalf of Mr. Coltman.'

She glanced round again. The shelves of books lining the walls with their frightening titles. *Policiers de roman et de laboratoire; Kriminalanthropolgie und Kriminalistik; Kriminalistische; Polizeihund und Jurisprudenz*; and authors with names like Wulffen; Reik; Stammler; Hiss; Kurz; Rumpf; and many others. She had recollected how once she had noticed that one bookcase had its glazed doors locked. She recalled asking Dr. Morelle the reason for this precaution and his reply which had sent chills crawling down her spine. And she remembered how once when her morbid curiosity had overcome her fear she had tried to glimpse the titles of the thick dossiers behind the glass, to discover that they bore only index-numbers, and how she had thought that the contents were not really frightening at all, that Dr. Morelle's answer to her question had been another example of his warped sense of humour. But even if she had possessed the key she would not have opened the bookcase for a thousand pounds.

'I hope you don't mind my calling on you like this,' Miss Frayle said. 'It's rather nice seeing you again. It seems ages since I last sat in this chair with my notebook.'

'I must admit I had noticed the passage of time myself,' Dr. Morelle said.

'Why I came to see you,' Miss Frayle said, 'is that — the idea's Mr. Coltman's — is that you should come down and talk to the students. On melodrama, its psychological origins. That sort of thing. It's the end of term next week, and we'd all be terribly thrilled if you would come, Dr. Morelle. I'm sorry to have called so late as this about it, but — '

'It doesn't happen to be the case, I suppose,' Dr. Morelle had said, 'that your Hugo Coltman has been let down at the last moment? I observed in this evening's newspaper that Sir Richard Kane has had to leave the cast of the play in which he has been appearing, owing to illness. I seem to remember he's a patron of your academy of drama.'

Miss Frayle blushed. She might have known that she would not get away with it, that Dr. Morelle, with his uncanny intuition, would have hit on the real reason behind this last-minute invitation.

'However,' she had heard Dr. Morelle say, 'you may tell Mr. Coltman that I accept his invitation,' and she brightened at once, and omitted to notice Dr. Morelle's enigmatic expression as his glance flickered over her.

2

Now Dr. Morelle smiled to himself slightly, rested his glance on Miss Frayle briefly as he recalled his own ulterior motive for accepting the invitation. She had said that the present Drama Workshop term was ending. Might she not come to him at least for part of the holidays? And once back working for him again, mightn't he be able to persuade her to remain, as in the old days?

The rich, theatrical voice in Dr. Morelle's ear went on.

'Dr. Morelle is, as you are aware, noted in several fields. His medical work is widespread, and as a criminologist he has been consulted by the police authorities in America and Europe, besides our own Scotland Yard.'

Dr. Morelle brought his thoughts back to the talk he was about to give. He would begin with an analysis of the psychological implications of melodrama;

the preoccupation of the human race with death; the Latin countries with their bullfighting, the Anglo-Saxons with blood sports. He would move on to the story of George Barnwell, the seventeenth-century apprentice who had been hanged for murder, and whose brief history had been the basis for ballads of the time and plays, which had been performed and plagiarized all over Europe.

A burst of applause was Dr. Morelle's cue to rise as Hugo Coltman sat down. It was then that it happened. A sharp splintering sound, as two legs of the chair collapsed, and Coltman fell heavily on the stage with the wreck beneath him.

A moment of shocked silence, then the students' nervous laughter was cut short by Hugo Coltman's strangled growl of rage as, assisted by Dr. Morelle, he scrambled to his feet.

In the glare of his protuberant eyes Dr. Morelle saw something of the tyrannical temper which had caused him to be feared in his days as an actor-manager.

Miss Frayle could hardly believe her eyes as she jumped to her feet. Heavens, she thought, it's like some slap-stick film. She hurried up the steps at the side of the stage. She glanced back at the teachers, who stood indecisively, and at the rows of students, their sheepish grins fading.

'Mr. Coltman, this is awful. Dr. Morelle, I'm so sorry.' She turned back to Hugo Coltman, who was dusting his trousers, and pushing aside the shattered chair with his foot. He glared at her, his mouth working. For a moment she hesitated, fearful that he was about to blame her for what had happened. But after all she was only his secretary, and really it was hardly her job to protect him from practical jokers. She began talking rapidly.

'I'm sure I can explain what happened,' she said. 'This chair is a stage-property. It's being used in a play. By some awful mistake, it must have got mixed up with the real chairs, when the students were rehearsing this morning.'

She broke off, Dr. Morelle was eyeing her stonily. Coltman's gaze was less baleful. It was as if he was grateful to her for supplying an explanation which was more satisfactory to his wounded dignity than that he had been the object of a deliberate attempt to humiliate him before his own students.

'I am prepared to accept your explanation,' he said. A student came up on to the stage with another chair, and set it down for him. Dr. Morelle stood aside, meditatively watching Miss Frayle and the young man remove the broken chair into the wings.

Then Hugo Coltman was saying:

'I must apologize for this stupid interruption, Dr. Morelle. Please carry on.' Slowly and gingerly, Hugo Coltman sat down again, while Miss Frayle, as she returned to her place in the auditorium, could almost hear everybody holding their breath.

Dr. Morelle began speaking, carrying his audience along with him from his opening words, while Miss Frayle collected her thoughts.

What she had told Hugo Coltman, her hasty invention designed to reassure him that the ridiculous accident had not been a personal attack directed against him, or his distinguished guest, had been good enough for the moment.

But now she recalled undercurrents among the Drama Workshop's teachers, a rising resentment of their chief's domineering behaviour, which during the past term seemed to have increased. Was it this that had lain at the root of her earlier uneasiness?

She glanced involuntarily in the direction of Willard and Sullivan. They appeared, she thought, to be giving their attention completely to Dr. Morelle. But Elspeth Finch? And Roy Allen? She looked across at the other side of the theatre to see if either of the teachers had joined a group sitting there, but her brief glance did not discover them, before the shrill blast of a whistle made her jump. It halted Dr. Morelle, Hugo Coltman sat up as if he had been shot, and heads jerked back.

The noise came from directly above. Someone was outside the window over Miss Frayle, she glimpsed a fantastic figure capering outside on the balcony. Many of the students were jumping to

14

their feet. Hugo Coltman had come forward to the footlights to stare incredulously upwards. Dr. Morelle remained where he was, one eyebrow raised sardonically as he looked up.

There was a cackle of laughter from above.

'Did you see?' somebody gasped near Miss Frayle. 'A sort of hooded figure — '

Miss Frayle saw the robed, hooded apparition. Then the figure, seemingly faceless under the hood, reached in through the window. One of the large bowls of flowers toppled and fell.

It hurtled down, followed by a shower of petals, and a girl student screamed and flung herself aside. The bowl shattered to pieces on the floor. Pandemonium filled the theatre for a few moments, then Hugo Coltman's voice was raised peremptorily, harsh with anger.

'Control yourselves, everybody. Keep still.'

Miss Frayle was already hurrying in the direction of the staircase leading to the balcony above. Her heart was fluttering excitedly, she had the wild idea that she might catch the culprit.

'Miss Frayle — ' Hugo Coltman started to shout, but she did not hear him.

Dr. Morelle turned to Coltman. 'Please allow her to go. It is possible she might bring us some useful information.'

Calmly he lit a Le Sphinx, and the other turned to him.

'I must apologize to you again, Dr. Morelle. These monstrous happenings, never in all my experience — ' He broke off, his mouth a thin line of some perplexity. 'I have insisted always on strict discipline,' he said. 'It is imperative in dealing with the variety of temperament found here, understandable temperament when one considers — '

'Quite,' Dr. Morelle said suavely. Thoughtfully he added, his gaze ranging over the restless students: 'Some silly young student, no doubt, inspired by the instinct for self-dramatization.'

'Whoever is responsible for this attempt to wreck this afternoon,' Hugo Coltman said, 'will be kicked out.'

Meanwhile, Miss Frayle had raced

upstairs, and along the corridor, through the door at the end which led on to the balcony. She halted suddenly, her heart leaping, as she heard somebody else running almost soundlessly, it seemed to her, behind her. She spun round on her heels.

It was Roy Allen, his black, springing hair untidy as usual.

'I saw you dash out,' he said. 'Quick of you to catch on, it's obvious the joker wasn't someone in the theatre.'

'That's what I thought,' said Miss Frayle.

They hurried along until they reached the window, still open, and through which they could hear the audience below.

There was no one in sight on the balcony.

'We're too late,' Miss Frayle said.

3

Roy Allen was looking at her curiously, his hands pushed deep in the pockets of his jacket.

'What exactly was going on? I must admit I wasn't listening very intently to the trick-cyclist. I was jotting down some notes.' He brought a crumpled paper from his pocket. 'Then I heard that fantastic noise. One of the students must have gone crazy.'

'Somebody has,' Miss Frayle said. She continued round the wide balcony. Then she heard an exclamation from Allen. He had pounced on a bundle jammed behind one of the open windows.

'What on earth's this doing here?'

It was a rough brown friar's robe, with a large hood.

'He was wearing it,' she said excitedly. 'No wonder his face was so well hidden.'

'*His* face?' Allen said. 'It was a man, then?'

Miss Frayle hesitated. 'It — it might even have been a woman, but I'm almost sure I glimpsed trousers.'

'Everyone here's got some idea of acting,' Allen said, 'it shouldn't be hard for anybody to put on that shrieking voice.'

They heard footsteps, and Jeff Sullivan came towards them, his eyes twinkling in his keen, sun-tanned face.

'Old Hugo's hopping mad,' he said. He spotted the robe. 'What's that?'

Miss Frayle and Allen explained, and he shrugged. 'Some damn fool practical joke. I don't see why Hugo's making such a fuss about it.'

'He might have been injured,' Miss Frayle said. 'That girl narrowly escaped being hit by the flower bowl.'

'I suppose so,' Sullivan said. 'Let's go down.'

The students, still excited and chattering, were dispersing to class-rooms, but a group of teachers was gathered round Hugo Coltman and Dr. Morelle, as Miss Frayle and the others reached the stage.

Coltman's anger overflowed when Miss

Frayle showed him the friar's robe: 'The Friar Laurence robe,' he said. 'The fool who wore it knew where to find it in the wardrobe,' he said. 'I intend to discover who it was.'

Theodore Willard, his thinning hair gleaming smoothly on his narrow head, said: 'Most of the students know their way around the wardrobe.'

'I shall question every one,' Hugo Coltman said. He threw a look at those around him. Miss Frayle felt the others stiffen with resentment at Coltman's implication that one of them might have been involved.

'If you'll forgive me,' Dr. Morelle said. 'But I must be returning to London. So much work to do.' He sighed, with an oblique glance at Miss Frayle. 'And nobody at present to help me.'

Coltman turned to him quickly and full of apologies he led Dr. Morelle away. Miss Frayle, blinking at the stiff group about her, followed hesitantly in the wake of Dr. Morelle.

Dr. Morelle halted, turning to look at the house in the lazy sunlight, rambling and many-windowed, a hotch-potch of Georgian and Victorian architecture and, attached to it, the circular theatre. His gaze ranged over the gardens, the wooded grounds, in which the Coltman Drama Workshop was set.

Miss Frayle watched him as he said good-bye to Hugo Coltman and got into his car, the familiar yellow, rakish Duesenberg convertible. She glanced at Hugo Coltman, who had moved back towards the house, then turned to Dr. Morelle.

'If there are any further developments, Miss Frayle,' he said to her quietly, 'I should be interested to hear from you.'

'You mean,' she said, 'something else may happen?'

Dr. Morelle shrugged non-committally and let in the clutch. His gaze flickered in Coltman's direction. 'He accepted your explanation that the broken chair was an accident.' He did not think it necessary to mention that he had noticed that both legs of the chair which had collapsed beneath Coltman had been sawn half-way through.

Miss Frayle watched the car turn out of the tall gates at the end of the short, gravel drive and head for London, some thirty miles distant. She saw Hugo Coltman's figure disappear beneath the porch and into the house.

Thoughtfully Miss Frayle wandered back to the house. Somebody must dislike Hugo Coltman, she thought to herself, and actively. She recalled the scene on the stage, the ripple of amusement from the students, that had greeted Coltman's discomfiture, as he had sprawled amidst the broken chair, amusement that had been quickly stilled by the sight of that furious figure, and the sound of that rage-filled voice.

Miss Frayle was still filled with misgivings as she went through the hall. She heard voices in the common-room and went in and found herself precipitated into a bitter hostile scene.

4

Jeff Sullivan was there, Elspeth Finch sat by Roy Allen, who looked gloomy and sullen. Theodore Willard was saying: 'He must be going off his head. I've been suspecting that he suffers from megalomania.'

Jeff Sullivan laughed. 'You'd be inclined to be upset yourself, if you'd just fallen with a wallop through a gag chair in full view of your students.'

'Theo never had much good to say for him,' Elspeth said.

'I say what I think,' Willard said, 'I don't kow-tow to Coltman or anyone else.'

'For God's sake, give it a rest,' Sullivan said, 'I'm tired of your yack-yack.'

Miss Frayle was studying him, in the electric atmosphere. By all accounts, he had knocked about before he had found himself at the Workshop. He was popular with the students, always good-humoured and ready for a joke. A joke, she thought suddenly. Surely it wasn't he who had carried out that fantastic practical joke in the theatre?

No, she decided. Against the man who was after all employing him and paying him? No, it didn't fit in.

Roy Allen broke into her thoughts. He was looking up at her curiously from under his brows. She noticed he had edged away from Elspeth Finch.

'What did the great Dr. Morelle think of it?'

Miss Frayle blushed, as all eyes turned on her. 'A stupid joke, that's all,' she said. 'Some high-spirited student, showing off.'

'That's what I say,' Roy Allen said. 'There's enough temperament flying around this place, without everybody throwing sinister glances at everybody else.'

'I agree with Roy,' said Elspeth Finch.

'Naturally,' Willard said, and she glanced at him with a faint smile. She turned to Sullivan.

'Talking of who was, or who was not in the theatre at the time,' she said, 'where was our Isobel?'

24

Isobel Ross. Miss Frayle had quite forgotten her. No doubt there had been malice in Elspeth's sudden introduction of her name, but Miss Frayle could not help recalling that she, too, had seen no sign of Isobel Ross in the theatre.

Jeff Sullivan was contemplating Elspeth, for once tense and unsmiling, his eyes veiled. 'What exactly do you mean by that, Elspeth?'

'We've been trying to work out who *wasn't* in the place. I'm sure I didn't see Isobel.'

Her small smooth head, with its shining black hair plaited neatly always, was held proudly. No doubt, Miss Frayle was thinking, some frustrated ambition had turned sour in her, but she moved with grace; as teacher of mime and movement she was highly competent. She was no longer young, but she could be attractive, were it not for the hard glint in her brown eyes, and the tightness of her small mouth.

Theodore Willard said thoughtfully: 'Now that's very interesting. I shouldn't have thought it, but Isobel — '

Isobel Ross walked into the common-room. 'What have I done now?'

As always, Miss Frayle, only too well aware of her own tendency to flutter, could not fail to admire Isobel Ross's serenity. She was not pretty. Straight-nosed, classical features, her curling auburn hair and cool green eyes, and her creamy skin. Not pretty, Miss Frayle thought, but very attractive. Once, she had said to Miss Frayle:

'I became quite sure early in my career my name would never be up in lights. Suppose I'm a teacher at heart. I'm happy passing on what I know to beginners. And there's always the thrill and excitement of finding genuine talent.'

She looked calmly at them now. Elspeth Finch, her thin red-tipped fingers clasped tightly, said lightly:

'We were just wondering where you'd been all afternoon.'

'Is it of interest to anybody?'

'We've all become amateur detectives,' Jeff Sullivan said, relaxed again, 'trying to discover who made Hugo sit down too suddenly and wrecked his afternoon for him.'

'I heard the students talking about it,'

Isobel Ross glanced at Willard. 'So you think I was prancing about on the theatre-roof, and hurling flower-pots about?' Her eyes shifted to Elspeth. 'Actually I was in my room all afternoon.' She gave Miss Frayle a smile. 'With all due respect to Dr. Morelle I thought I'd be doing better getting on with some work instead of listening to him.'

There was a silence. Then Elspeth said:

'You see, it was someone who knew their way around, and who wasn't in the theatre.'

'I can assure you it wasn't I,' Isobel said. 'As it happened the reason I wasn't in the theatre was because I was looking up a play for young Brian Wickham.'

'You show a great deal of interest in him, Isobel,' Willard said, and Miss Frayle thought his sidelong glance left no doubt about his insinuation.

'He's got talent,' Isobel said.

'Bit highly-strung, I've always thought,' Sullivan said.

'He does drive himself too hard,' Isobel said. 'He's got a talent for concentration, useful quality for anybody taking up a stage career.'

'Anyway you'll have to convince Hugo with your alibi,' Jeff Sullivan said. 'His idea is to get us in one after the other, shine strong lights into our eyes and force a confession from one of us.'

'He won't bother me,' Isobel said. 'My conscience is clear. How's yours, Theo?'

'What d'you mean?' Willard looked at her sharply. 'Why pick on me?'

'You've never been exactly friendly with Hugo, have you?'

'What rubbish are you saying?' Willard said and turned as if to bluster from the room.

'No more rubbish than your suspecting me: or,' Isobel added, 'than your insinuation that I'm infatuated with Brian Wickham.'

Isobel Ross spun on her heel and went out quickly. After a pause, Willard went out next, followed by Elspeth Finch, then Sullivan who grinned at Miss Frayle. Roy Allen was last out before Miss Frayle, who stood gazing after them all.

Isobel Ross, she was deciding, was

certainly the first person she had come across that afternoon who had definitely *not* been in the theatre at the time of the commotion. But was she so sure about Sullivan, Willard, Elspeth Finch, and Roy Allen? At one time or another, she had missed all of them; while she had been absorbed in Dr. Morelle's talk for instance, she'd had eyes for no one but him.

There might not be any clues to the perpetrator of the mad joke, it occurred to her, but there was certainly no lack of suspects.

5

Brian Wickham sat on the broad window-sill of the room where Isobel Ross took her classes. The late afternoon sunlight poured through the windows, this room was in the oldest part of the great house. Panelled walls, around which ran shelf above shelf of the plays of dramatists ranging from Shakespeare to Shaw, from Marlowe to Noel Coward.

There was peace here, away from his small, cramped home in the little Surrey market-town half a mile away on the slopes of the Hog's Back. Yet to-day the peace had been shattered, and he felt keenly the undercurrent of suspense that had rippled through the Coltman Drama Workshop.

'Mugging up a part, or just dreaming of seeing your name in neons?'

Wickham started, then smiled at the round-faced cheerful youth who had come into the room.

'You still here, Dicky?' he said. 'I thought you'd packed off home for tea. I've never known you miss your food.'

Dicky Bennett was his cousin, a year or so younger than himself. Dicky also lived locally, but in a much larger house, his parents were well-off, and he took his studies less seriously. He was talented, but in a more superficial way than Brian; he excelled in light comedy. Brian was equipped for intense romantic and dramatic rôles.

'Been home once,' Dicky said. 'Forgot that script I'm studying for next Friday's do, and had to come back for it. I met your mother on the way. She asked me if you were still here.'

Wickham's mother had scrimped and saved to get him to the Workshop. His father, who had been a concert-pianist, with a future full of promise, was killed before Brian had been born, at the Rhine crossing. Brian had obtained one of the scholarships offered by Hugo Coltman, and that alone had enabled him to study acting at all. That, plus the fact that he happened to live locally and so did not

31

have to face the expense of travelling to and from a London dramatic academy.

'I suppose I must go,' he said. But he made no further move. Instead: 'By the way, Dicky, has anyone any idea who did it?'

Dicky shook his head. 'Not a clue.' He grinned, 'It was great fun, wasn't it?'

'Coltman didn't think it was so funny. I thought,' he went on, frowning thoughtfully, 'that whoever it was might have been boasting about it among the rest of the students. Come to think, though, I wonder if it was one of us at all? Somehow it doesn't strike me as that sort of trick.'

Dicky's blue eyes bulged a little. He sat on the window-sill and faced the other.

'Who else could it have been? You don't think it was one of the teachers?' He broke off and the grin spread across his face. 'Imagine old Willard leaping about on the roof, or Finch.'

'No, of course,' Wickham said. 'But it's a queer business. I've had a funny feeling lately that something was brewing.'

'Turning all psychic, are you?' His

cousin stared at Wickham's thin face, with its mobile and expressive dark eyes. Old Brian thought too much, he decided. He flogged his brain too hard. 'Sounds a bit peculiar to me,' he said, 'sensing trouble before it comes. See anything else in your crystal?'

Brian Wickham told himself he shouldn't have spoken of it to Dicky, the light-hearted extrovert. He wouldn't understand. Not that he himself could understand the premonitions that had filled him the last few weeks. The uneasy conviction that something was wrong. He glanced at his cousin, as the other gave an exclamation. 'I say,' he said, 'how about us trying to track down the blighter?'

It was something they could do, Dicky went on enthusiastically, to try and forestall any further trouble. 'Could you round up one or two chaps?'

'What for?'

'In case whoever it was is planning any more of these tricks,' Dicky said. 'Forewarned is fore-something-or-other, and all that. You don't mix much, but I'm always moving around, and one or two others might pick up a tip, and the funny man could be nipped in the bud.'

'But do you think that's quite necessary?' Brian said. 'I mean it was only a practical joke, after all. There's no reason why it should happen again.'

'It came within an ace of being serious,' Dicky Bennett said.

Brian nodded. It might have been a nasty business. 'What would have happened if the bowl had fallen on someone's head?' He thought there might be something in the idea, after all.

'The idea is to form a sort of practical joke patrol,' Dicky said. 'Sherlock Bennett and his Baker Street Scouts on the trail. What about the girls?' He began to sound even more enthusiastic. 'Sonia for instance, she always knows what's going on ages before anybody else.' He grinned, thinking of his particular girl-friend of the moment and her lively curiosity.

'Better not get too many,' Brian said. 'Or it's sure to leak out.' His face clouded. 'Perhaps we're being stupid, perhaps it isn't such a good idea. There won't be any more funny business.'

'You think there will be really, the tea-leaves at the bottom of your cup tell you so,' Dicky said. 'After all, it all helps us to take our minds off our work. Think over my scheme.'

Dicky Bennett went away a few minutes later, whistling. Soon Brian slid off the window-sill and crossed to the shelves to get a book. As he walked along the quiet corridor to leave for his home, he heard footsteps descending the stairs, and Isobel Ross joined him in the wide entrance hall, and her eyes searched his face.

'I find it difficult to leave,' he said to her. 'It's so quiet here.'

'Wouldn't do you any harm to spend a little time outdoors,' she said.

She walked across to the wide panelled door, Wickham behind her. As she put out her hand to the catch, he opened the door for her and stood aside to let her pass. There was the click of heels behind them, and an acid voice jarred in their ears.

'Enjoying your tête-à-tête? But don't keep your pupil from his work too long, Isobel.'

And Elspeth Finch brushed past them both and swept through the doorway.

6

It was Hugo Coltman's custom to assemble his staff and the pupils every morning in the theatre, before work for the day started, which was at nine o'clock. By this time, those students who lived locally had arrived to mingle with the other students who lived in the old house, which had been suitably converted. There were dormitories and sitting-rooms and a large dining-hall; as well as accommodation for those members of the staff who lived in the house.

These morning pep-talks offered Coltman the opportunity to project his undoubtedly vivid personality, to cement his dominance over students and staff. Secretly, Miss Frayle thought that he was a bit of a bore about it.

On the morning following Dr. Morelle's visit to the Drama Workshop, Miss Frayle hovered at the back of the theatre, as Hugo Coltman came on to the empty stage. With her were Jeff Sullivan, Elspeth Finch, Willard and Isobel Ross. Roy Allen stood by himself on the other side of the theatre. Miss Frayle noticed how Elspeth's eyes would drift in his direction. She turned to watch while Hugo Coltman sent his gaze moving along each row of students, pausing here and there on a particular youth or girl, who stirred restlessly as his look held them.

His face looked haggard, Miss Frayle thought. There were pouches under his eyes. It was plain that he was still labouring under a strong emotion, that he had by no means forgotten the previous day's fiasco. The students sat down, and there was a scuffling and scraping of feet.

'I do not intend to say much about yesterday's occurrence. The facts speak for themselves. I will say this, however, that whoever was responsible for what happened is someone I do not intend shall remain here, at my Drama Workshop.'

Miss Frayle thought she could catch a

movement, an intake of breath on all sides. Had Hugo Coltman found out who it was?

'I have built up this school of acting and training for the theatre upon a tradition of discipline. I propose to take steps this morning towards discovering the identity of the culprit.'

Now Miss Frayle caught a sigh of anticipation from the auditorium. She saw Coltman's massive head thrust forward, he stood poised as if about to swoop down upon some prey he had singled out for attack.

'You will all return to your various classrooms. You will then, each one of you, write an account of your movements during yesterday afternoon, in particular noting anything which upon reflection you consider may have had any bearing upon the disgraceful happenings in this theatre at the time.'

Miss Frayle frowned to herself. But he's asking them to spy on each other, she thought. Surely that isn't right? It is more likely to cause further trouble.

'You will sign your notes,' Coltman

said. 'And they will be collected by your teachers and brought to me.'

Hugo Coltman turned on his heel and stalked from the stage. Then, as the students automatically began to move out of the theatre, the murmur of their conversation rose more and more loudly.

'Crikey,' Miss Frayle heard Jeff Sullivan say inelegantly, 'he must have lain awake all night dreaming up that one.'

'I refuse to have anything to do with it,' Theodore Willard said. 'I absolutely refuse to have anything to do with it.'

Some two hours later Miss Frayle was in her office. Her desk was already becoming hidden by the papers brought in by the teachers, as the students followed Hugo Coltman's instructions and made notes of their movements during the previous afternoon and any observations that they thought appropriate.

Miss Frayle had glanced at some of the students' outpourings. Some were lengthy, some were brief. Some had been written in meticulous hands, some scrawled. Some of the writers had carried out their task with deadly seriousness, others with obvious levity. Miss Frayle decided that Hugo Coltman's idea would turn out to be a complete waste of time. All this, and her horn-rims swept the overcrowded desk, was calculated merely to aggravate him.

The door opened and Elspeth Finch came in, carrying a handful of papers.

'Here's my batch,' she said. 'I had to be very firm with the students in the interests of discipline, but I don't expect much light to come from all this rubbish.'

'Oh, I don't know,' Miss Frayle said, 'there might be just a hint.'

'You're not working for Dr. Morelle now,' Elspeth said. 'I should have thought this detective stuff should be carried out by proper people.'

She walked out, leaving Miss Frayle to sort out all the papers and check them to make sure that they all bore the names of the writers.

Elspeth Finch went along to the staff common room. It was empty except for the solitary figure of Roy Allen. He was engrossed over some sheets of music manuscript. Her eyes lit up, and she went towards him.

'Hello, Roy. Busy?'

The sharpness had gone from her voice. It was warm and friendly.

He looked up abstractedly from his manuscript. 'Didn't hear you come in,' he said casually.

Speculatively he stared at her for a moment, then returned to the symbols he had scrawled on the paper. She stood gazing down at the dark, bent head, all her longing for him in her expression. She caught her breath with almost a physical pang, and colour warmed her pale features.

'My lot have just finished their notes for Hugo,' she said brightly.

Roy's pen stopped. 'What a crazy scheme,' he said. 'Typical of that pompous ass.'

Glad to have this chance of talking to him alone, Elspeth went on: 'I'm not so sure it mightn't produce something, as a matter of fact.'

'My dear woman, you don't imagine the guilty fool will write the truth about himself or herself, do you?' His tone was deliberately rude. Her hands clenched. 'Don't you imagine an alibi was fixed before the thing happened, yesterday?' he said. 'This whole business is a stupid waste of time.'

He laughed cynically, and she leaned forward, impulsively, putting a hand on his arm.

'Roy, don't laugh at me, please! You may be right . . . you probably are. Why should we worry, anyway? It's Hugo's headache.'

Her unusual humility, the pleading in her voice brought a wary light to his eyes. He glanced at her sharply, his expression cold. What game was she playing now? These were new tactics. She still gripped his arm.

'I wish you didn't dislike me,' she said. 'What have I done?'

He regarded her coldly. 'What on earth are you talking about?' he said. He shook her hand off his arm.

'Just because I don't normally make a parade of my feelings,' she said, 'you think I haven't any.'

'Should I have the faintest interest in your feelings?' he said, calculated brutality in his voice.

Elspeth reeled as if he had struck her a physical blow. He made as if to move towards her, fearing she was about to faint. Then he restrained himself.

'Please,' she said, her voice was thick. 'I'm not making this up. You do behave as though you don't like me, and I'm asking you why.'

'Don't dramatize yourself,' he said. 'Leave that to your students. I've too much on my mind to worry about liking or disliking you. Why on earth this sudden outburst, anyway?'

'Because — ' She fought to control the trembling in her voice. 'Because I suddenly felt it was important to me to know.'

He could see her whole body shivering, and a wave of horrified pity swept through him. She turned to the window. He guessed it was because she wanted to hide her emotions.

'I haven't many friends here, my life isn't much fun. I seem to spend all my free time looking after my mother. Sometimes I get so worked up I don't know what I'm doing. I feel that people here — that you — hate me.'

Her voice was rising hysterically. She was not far from tears. Roy Allen held back his impatience with her for having precipitated a scene in which he was not in the least interested.

'Sorry, Elspeth,' he said more mildly. 'Didn't mean to snap at you. But, if you want the truth, how can you expect to be popular, the way you snarl at everybody?'

Her face was working, her eyes bright. He saw her knuckles whiten as she clenched her hands together.

'I can't help it,' she said, her voice shaking with emotion. 'Sometimes the students drive me silly. Isobel and Sullivan do nothing but make fun of me. Roy, what can I do?'

In one swift movement she was beside him, her brown eyes peering hungrily into his face, her fingers clutching his arm.

He felt a shock of distaste. Why must she inflict her neuroses on him? He shrugged, saying: 'What can I say

— except to suggest you try to make yourself more pleasant to people.'

Elspeth flinched visibly as his advice struck home. She stiffened and drew back, staring angrily at him.

'So you're on their side as well, are you?' And then she burst out: 'I'm not so unattractive as you think. There is someone anyway — '

'Oh, shut up, for God's sake,' Allen said, interrupting her, his patience vanishing. 'If you've got someone in tow, why pester me?' His tone was disbelieving as he said it.

'Roy — darling.'

'Leave me in peace,' he said. 'I've got work to do. You come butting in with your stupid scenes.'

Breathless, on the edge of hysteria, her face contorted. Then, her teeth showing, she snatched the music manuscript from him.

'You haven't tried to help me,' she said. 'I asked you, out of them all, but I won't be insulted by you.'

With a furious exclamation he leaped at her, trying to grab the manuscript, but her hands were already crumpling the top sheet.

'Blast you, give that to me,' he said harshly.

She backed away, and he gripped her arm. Grimly, he tried to force open her fingers, his face convulsed with anger as he stared into the triumphant, smiling face so near his own.

'That's the only copy, give it to me, you lunatic.'

It seemed that her grip would never relax, but suddenly, staring into his young, distorted face, Elspeth opened her hands so that the crumpled paper dropped to the floor. Before he could bend to pick it up, her thin arms were round his neck, and her mouth was pressed to his.

He stood there, rigid, in sheer surprise.

'You know I'm fond of you,' she said. 'I'd do anything for you.'

Disgust showed in his face. With a grunt of anger he tried to push her away.

At that moment the door opened and Theodore Willard and Jeff Sullivan walked in. For a moment, nobody moved or spoke, then Willard, his eyes glittering, smoothing his thin hair and with a forced smile on his narrow face, said: 'Which play is this you're rehearsing, Elspeth?'

Her face crimson, she turned away from Roy.

'I hate you,' she said. 'I hate you all.'

Her heels beating a tattoo on the floor, she ran swiftly out of the room, slamming the door behind her.

7

Jeff Sullivan was grinning, while Willard turned as the door slammed on the embarrassed silence that had followed their entrance upon the scene between Allen and Elspeth Finch. 'She's certainly fallen for you in a big way,' Sullivan said.

Roy Allen laughed uncomfortably. 'I gave her no encouragement.'

Willard had turned back to him. 'That's what you say,' he said.

Jeff Sullivan thought he detected an odd note in the other's tone, then decided he was mistaken. 'Why not make the most of it?' he said to Allen. 'She could be attractive, if she controlled her tongue. I'll bet there's some fire there.'

'Frankly, I think it's rather disgusting, Sullivan,' Theodore Willard said. 'After all, she's not a young woman.'

Roy Allen was picking up his music. A trifle uneasily he said: 'I'd appreciate it if you didn't mention it to anyone. I hope

Elspeth sees what a fool she's made of herself.'

Jeff Sullivan shrugged. 'No business of mine, old chap.'

'Let's forget it,' Willard said. He moved to the door. 'That fool Hugo's been asking for me.'

'Edgier than ever, that chap,' Sullivan said to Allen as Theodore Willard went out. He was thinking again of that strange note in Willard's voice, and he began wondering why it was the other showed such animosity towards Hugo Coltman. It was almost as if he felt some deep-seated grudge against his employer. Sullivan sighed inwardly. He'd be thankful when the term ended, and he could get away from the Drama Workshop. Suddenly he found himself wondering if he'd ever come back to the place.

A little while later Willard stamped angrily into Miss Frayle's office. Looking up from her desk Miss Frayle saw storm signals in his heightened colour and glittering eyes.

'Whatever is the matter, Mr. Willard?'

'I hope his blasted school crumbles

about his ears,' Willard said. 'I won't put up with much more of it, Miss Frayle. I've just about had enough.' He strode up and down restlessly.

'What's Mr. Coltman done now?'

'He's only called me over the coals for what he pompously refers to as contravention of his orders, in refusing to agree to his stupid notion about the students writing out notes concerning yesterday afternoon. I told my students to ignore the whole thing.'

Miss Frayle was taken aback. 'You can hardly blame Mr. Coltman then,' she said, 'for being annoyed with you. It will ruin the whole thing.' She indicated the papers on her desk. 'It makes the rest of these useless.'

'Damned good job, too,' Willard said. 'Of all the stupid ideas he's ever dreamed up, that's the worst. I told him so, and he didn't like it.'

Miss Frayle looked worried. 'Is there any sense in making him more angry?'

'I'm not worried if it does,' Willard smiled triumphantly. 'At first he went all wounded dignity. But then he changed his act. He started to roar in his best melodrama voice. There was no point, he said, in discussing the matter further. Lord knows what was brewing in that mind of his. He'll come down on me in some way.'

And quite right, too, Miss Frayle thought to herself. What an odious man he can be, she felt, blinking at Willard.

'I'd give anything to see that soaring pride of his deflated,' Willard said. 'That's a day worth waiting for. This blessed school of his — his noble Drama Workshop. There's nothing so wonderful about it, but by the way he talks you'd think there was no other drama-school like it in the world. I tell you, a few more incidents like yesterday's would shake him up a bit. That was really funny, the way he collapsed with that chair.'

His laugh was venomous. Miss Frayle stared round-eyed through her glasses at him. He was certainly revealing his own mean mind and petty soul. With such hate towards Hugo Coltman, his boss, was it possible that Theodore Willard himself had perpetrated the insane trick?

Then, she thought, would he have talked so revealingly to herself and the others? Unless it was a cunning way of diverting suspicion from himself?

'I don't think you should talk like this, Mr. Willard,' she said. 'I certainly don't want to see any more trouble here. It was a wretched business, and I hope they catch whoever did it, and — and punish them severely.'

'Defending your noble employer, naturally,' Willard said. 'Let me tell you they won't find the joker. And I say again: I hope whoever it was thinks up more little tricks, it'll jerk Hugo Coltman out of his cosy, private world of vanity and self-esteem.'

'Coming from a member of Hugo Coltman's staff,' a cool voice said, 'that's a very charming sentiment.'

It was Isobel Ross who had come into the office and at the sound of her voice, Willard spun round.

'Nobody's asking you for your opinion,' he said. 'Though no doubt, if you had your way, you'd have me out on my ear.'

Isobel Ross shrugged. 'You'll get

yourself thrown out on your ear,' she said. 'Especially if you let Hugo hear you talking like that. I shouldn't do it, if I were you, he might start wondering.'

'Wondering what? What are you suggesting?'

'Anybody who says he'd like to see more incidents like the last might be the guilty party.'

'Why, you bitch,' Willard was livid and he moved towards Isobel. 'Take that back, or I'll damn well make you.'

Miss Frayle sprang up, a protest on her lips, but Isobel and Willard ignored her. Isobel's eyes sparkled furiously.

'What you said was disloyal and sounded pretty rotten from a paid member of the staff — '

To Miss Frayle's horror, Willard's hand swung round in a stinging slap, and she saw the red mark on Isobel's face.

'Very pretty.' It was another voice which broke in on the tense scene, a voice harsh and angry. 'Damn you, Theo, you get out of here — fast. Before I take you apart.'

Jeff Sullivan had come in, and he

grabbed Willard's arm fiercely. Willard shook his grip off. His gaze now fixed on Isobel's white face, with the mark of his blow blazing across it. At last he swung round, stared dumbly at Sullivan for a moment, then, at a shambling run, rushed out.

Sullivan took Isobel's arm, while Miss Frayle stood quite shocked and unable to speak or move for the moment. Isobel's energy seemed to have drained from her. She went rather unsteadily to a chair.

'He had a quarrel with Mr. Coltman,' Miss Frayle said to her and Jeff Sullivan, as if in explanation of Willard's behaviour. 'I think he said rather more than he meant. Really, he seems quite to have lost his head over the whole business. He said some awful things about Mr. Coltman and the Workshop.' Her face was troubled. Sullivan eyed her keenly, as she went on: 'He's said so much he's made himself the obvious suspect. I don't think he'd have done if — ' She let her words trail off uncertainly.

Her voice quite calm, Isobel Ross said: 'I don't see Willard lowering himself to enter into a plot with one of the students.'

Jeff Sullivan didn't say anything, and he and Isobel went off to their respective classes. Sullivan was trying to fathom the reason for Willard's dislike for Coltman. He could not help wondering that it was as if Willard was taking it out of old Hugo for no other reason than that he was being given a rough deal in some other quarter.

Isobel Ross, the marks of Willard's slap vanishing from her face, faced her students speculatively. What a mixed bunch they were. Miller, at the back there, would never grasp the meaning behind the words he spoke mechanically. Peggy Thomson was painstaking and hard-working, but without fire or colour.

Luckily they weren't all of the same calibre. There was young Wickham, who seemed to know by instinct, to absorb and transmute the words before him into rich emotion. Thank heavens for Wickham. A student like that made teaching worthwhile.

'We'll take the Seven Ages speech again. Wickham, perhaps you'd start.'

Brian Wickham rose to his feet.

'All the world's a stage,
And all the men and women merely players.
They have their exits and their entrances — '

Isobel Ross could not help looking at him in astonishment. He was declaiming in a flat, colourless voice, losing all the sense of rhythm of the words, and waving one hand mechanically. Now he broke off, frowning. He looked around him wildly.

'At first the infant — ' He broke off again. Again he tried, 'At first the infant — ' Again he stopped, passing a hand across his forehead in agitation.

'Wickham, whatever's the matter? You know every word of this by heart.' Isobel prompted him: 'At first the infant, Mewling and puking in the nurse's arms.'

He looked at her agonizedly.

'Miss Ross, I — I've forgotten, I've forgotten everything.'

He was staring at her, a strange expression in his eyes, the other students watching him curiously.

Isobel hastened to try and calm him, she saw by his haggard face and frightened expression that he had been seized by an unusual panic.

'You could never forget it,' she said. 'You've spoken it splendidly many a time. Don't worry, it'll come back. It's not uncommon to have a sudden dry-up. Even experienced actors go through that sort of thing, often.'

The other students grinned between themselves and relaxed. But Wickham, still on his feet, continued to stare at her tragically. For a moment she thought he was playing a trick, assuming an air of heavy drama.

'I'm sorry,' he said, thickly, at last. 'I can't think.' He suddenly slumped into a chair and buried his face in his hands.

'Wickham,' Isobel said sharply. 'Get a grip on yourself.'

He raised his head to look at her. A wave of apprehension swept over her. 'I'm sorry,' he said again. 'May someone else do it?'

Only two days before, Isobel was recalling, he had spoken these lines beautifully, with no halting, no searching of his memory. What was the matter with him to-day? Was he overtired, had he been driving himself too hard?

She said quietly: 'Very well. Miller, we'll hear you instead. You've been enjoying a pleasant doze in the corner.'

Brian Wickham sat dazed, staring ahead of him, chin propped in a hand. Isobel made no further attempt to include him in the lesson, guessing at the misery he must feel.

Wickham's brain was in a whirl. He had been reasonably proud of his unusual powers of memorizing and concentrating, the mechanics of acting. Taking for granted his never-failing fund of instinctive knowledge and his amazing memory, he had often been puzzled by the labour needed and the agony of mind endured by others in acquiring even a part of his skill.

Only recently, stirred by the admiration Isobel Ross had expressed for his work, had he begun to realize that his gifts were unusual. With this realization had come not greater pride, but a grateful humility for the powers that might help bring within his grasp the future he cherished.

To-day, though, his confidence seemed suddenly to have melted. The sure background of knowledge was swept away in a whirling darkness. He wondered wildly whether he was about to have a mental breakdown?

It occurred to him that perhaps he was more sensitive than others to the strange events in the theatre yesterday afternoon, and the unpleasantness that seemed to breathe the very air of the Drama Workshop. He tried to take a grip of his thoughts. He was letting his nerves get on top of him. He was behaving hysterically.

Alarmed and lonely, Brian Wickham sat hearing, not the lesson that proceeded around him, but the wild laughter of the prancing figure whose mockery had shattered Hugo Coltman's proud composure, whose presence seemed to threaten his own immediate future, as well as that of the Drama Workshop.

8

The fine spell that had started the previous week-end was still giving an illusion of summer. The town on the Hog's Back had basked in the warm sunshine all day. Now, it was nearly eleven o'clock at night, and the footsteps of the passers-by echoed on the pavement under Dicky Bennett's window.

He had been lying on top of his bed ruminating about the evening's tennis he had enjoyed with some of his friends, but now, roused by a burst of laughter under his window, he rolled off the bed and switched on the bedside-lamp.

From the pocket of his jacket he produced a bundle of papers. 'First bulletin from Bill Mead,' he read. 'Conversation overheard to-day.'

Bill Mead's scribble conveyed nothing that had anything to do with that business in the Workshop theatre. He was probably making most of it up anyway, Dicky

Bennett reflected; a pretty imaginative mind, Bill had. Impatiently he screwed up the papers. There was nothing to be learned from the amateur investigations he had set in motion. Dicky Bennett slid off his bed and looked out into the night. The moon was nearly full. Clicking off his light, he stood by the open window, his breathing suddenly quickening as an idea came to him.

It was a crime to be indoors, trying to sleep, on such a night. How far was it to the Drama Workshop? A few minutes on his bike.

Talking to Brian Wickham about it, he had thought only of keeping an eye and ear open during the daytime, but wasn't it more likely that anybody bent on mischief might set their plans when the place was deserted, when there was less fear of interruption?

In a more reasonable moment Dicky Bennett would have acknowledged the unlikelihood of any such thing, but here, in a room flooded by moonlight, as he looked out over the black-and-white patchwork of the street below, his heart beat faster at the thought.

In another moment he had put on rubber-soled shoes. The upturned collar of his jacket hid the whiteness of his shirt.

As he crept downstairs and through the kitchen, he grinned to himself. This was quite an adventure; it was, in fact, more for the adventure of the thing than because he believed he might find some clue to the mystery that activated him.

He padded to the garden shed, got his bicycle and wheeled it silently to the back gate. Soon, a swift shadow in the moonlight, he was pedalling towards the Drama Workshop. A faint breeze cooled his face and ruffled his hair as, presently, he coasted downhill, seeing the old house and its grounds below him.

He left his bike in the shadows against the wall, slipped through the wicket-gate, which creaked startlingly loud in the silence, and was heading across the grounds, in the ghostly light of the moon. For a moment, uncertainly, he paused, staring at the shadowed house.

Now he half regretted his idea, which had seemed such fun in the comfort and safety of his own home.

There was an eeriness, an air of waiting, about the rambling building, a silent watchfulness far removed from the cheerful bustle and clamour of the working day. Not a light showed anywhere.

He stepped off the path on to the grass, alarmed by the scrape of his own feet on the gravel, and approached a jutting wing of the building. There was a window with a broken latch in the gymnasium where Jeff Sullivan instructed his pupils, and previous experience had shown it to be easy enough to swing up on to the low window-ledge and drop through into the room.

He reached up and gripped the window-ledge. Then, muscles tensed for the thrust that would lift him up, he paused. He could hear his heart pounding unpleasantly.

The window was open already.

Had the caretaker neglected to fasten it? Or, he wondered, had someone else gone before him?

There the window was, anyway, wide

open to the night. For a moment Dicky Bennett hesitated. Then he asked himself hadn't he come to try and trap the joker? What was he waiting for? Still gripping the sill, he stood there, wondering whether to rouse everybody and chance making a fool of himself, or go in boldly, to stalk the unknown.

Curiosity winning, he sprang up. His feet scuffed on the surface of the wall, then one knee was on the sill, and the other followed.

Thinking that, if anyone within was waiting for him with a gun, what a target he must make outlined against the moonlight, he dropped quietly into the room. It was deserted and he could see that the door at the far end was shut.

He padded across the room and opened the door silently, looking out into the main corridor. His breath was coming faster now, and his heart thudded. Faint stirrings of air, rustlings, the hint of some unseen presence, made his skin crawl unpleasantly.

He took a deep breath and went towards the theatre. It was there that the antics which had attracted him here had occurred. Silently he passed through a dim, ghostly backstage. The air seemed coldest here, with draughts creeping around the stacked flats and drapes.

The curtain was up, and he stole across the stage, staring out into the moonlit auditorium. Moonlight streamed through the high window, the rays cutting down across the rows of seats.

Quietly, he went down the steps at the side of the stage, then suddenly he halted, and he was unable to restrain an audible gasp.

He was standing beside one of the fine oil paintings of Hugo Coltman in his past rôles. There he was, a younger man, in armour as Richard III. But the proud figure was now marred.

Dicky Bennett stared in horror. The streaming moonlight showed a frame in which the painting hung in tatters. This masterly portrait had been slashed insanely, across and across, the face, the armour, the sensitive hands, ripped and ruined.

Dicky Bennett moved on, to the next

painting. Hugo Coltman's *Macbeth*, a fine and tragic figure. That, too, had been slashed beyond recognition. Hugo Coltman as Hamlet, the dreaming eyes slashed across until they seemed like blind gaps in the fine face.

What ghastly thing had happened here to-night? What maniac had slashed in insane destruction at the pictures of Hugo Coltman? Dazed, Dicky Bennett moved on, then jumped, his heart thudding.

He had almost walked into an object that gleamed in the moonlight.

There, as he stood before the next magnificent painting of Coltman as King Lear, he saw the sword. It had been driven viciously into the heart of the painted figure, and protruded, quivering and glittering brightly. The writhing, contorted features of the mad old king, the sword driven to his painted heart gave a ghastly impression of a man mortally wounded, dying before Dicky Bennett's eyes.

He backed away, shaking with terror, and turned back to the stage and went up the steps.

He must tell Hugo Coltman. This was far worse than the first practical jokes. This was malicious damage, a deadly stroke aimed at Hugo Coltman.

He gained the stage, and then a cold chill of fear ran through him. The curtain nearest him on the prompt-corner side had stirred. He knew it was no draught this time. Someone was there in the darkness. Before he could turn, a hand clutched his shoulder. Another hand came round over his mouth, stifling his sudden cry.

He fought to tear himself away.

He heard sharp breathing, and next moment he was flung away violently by his unseen attacker. He staggered, tripped across the footlights, and felt himself falling.

He crashed into the orchestra pit, and a jarring pain, darkness and unconsciousness swept over him.

9

Miss Frayle heard the shriek, and after pausing to reassure herself that her ears had not deceived her she hurried out of her office.

It was eight-thirty, the morning was bright with the promise of another sunny day, and Miss Frayle had been putting in some work before breakfast. End of term approaching meant that there were all sorts of extra jobs to be taken care of, and Hugo Coltman was not as business-like as he might have been in administrative matters, with the result that Miss Frayle found herself having to deal with all sorts of items unexpectedly pushed on her in the rush.

There was no repetition of the cry which had startled her and which seemed to have come from the direction of the theatre. She went quickly through the old house and through the door at the end of the long hall. She started to hurry past the rows of long seats and then she stopped in her tracks for a moment as she saw the group of people on the stage. There was the general handyman, old Baxter, and the two women cleaners.

They were bent over a figure sprawled upon the stage. Old Baxter turned at Miss Frayle's approach. 'Student,' he said. 'Fallen into the orchestra.'

'He's dead,' one of the women said, and shook her head.

Miss Frayle gasped with horror, then relaxed as Baxter turned on the woman.

'Shut up,' he said. 'He's not dead. Had a bad bang, that's all. But his heart's beating all right.'

'Someone must have bashed him one,' the other woman said.

Miss Frayle ran up on to the stage. She saw that it was Dicky Bennett lying there in a twisted attitude. There was blood matting his hair and darkening one side of his chalk-white face.

'He was lying there,' the woman cleaner who had first spoken said. 'Give me a terrible turn when I saw him.'

'We got him up here,' Baxter said. 'I

was just going to let Mr. Coltman or someone know.'

'You haven't telephoned for a doctor?' Miss Frayle said.

Baxter shook his head. 'It took us a bit of time to shift him,' he said. 'And now you're here.'

It occurred to Miss Frayle that it would have been better if young Bennett had not been moved without a doctor seeing him first. And then it suddenly struck her: and the police, wouldn't they have preferred that the crumpled figure had been left as it was? A chill gripped her. Police, what made her think of them? Automatically she had connected this accident to young Bennett with the bad business the day before yesterday. And then: accident? she wondered. Was it an accident? What had one of the cleaners meant about having been bashed?

'You're sure he's alive?' she asked Baxter kneeling beside the inert figure. Baxter nodded emphatically.

'I can't understand how he came to be here at all,' she said. 'He's not one of the boarders, he ought to be at home.'

'Up to mischief,' Baxter said, 'I shouldn't wonder. Maybe thought that it would be a bit of a joke to come prowling — '

'Joke?' Miss Frayle said, her eyes wide behind her glasses. She stared down at the waxen face of Dicky Bennett, who lay there, breathing stertorously.

'Serves the little blighter right,' Baxter said. 'He shouldn't have come larking round.'

Had he missed his footing, Miss Frayle asked herself yet again, and injured himself accidentally? Or had he met some other furtive, crazed intruder, who had attacked him?

An outraged cry broke into her thoughts.

'We haven't seen the half of it yet.' It was one of the woman cleaners. 'Look at this. Anybody'd think there'd been a lunatic in here last night.'

Miss Frayle looked round, where the woman was staring at one of the paintings on the wall. She saw the sword sticking from the painted heart of King Lear.

Miss Frayle dashed down the steps to

the woman. The other woman cleaner had hurried away to telephone for the doctor.

'Dicky Bennett couldn't have done this,' Miss Frayle said. She glanced at Baxter on the stage. Then her gaze took in the slashed canvases.

'If the young devil did do this,' Baxter said from where he stood, 'I wouldn't like to be in his shoes when he recovers.'

'He might have caught somebody else,' Miss Frayle said. 'And that's how he got hurt.'

'In that case,' the man said, 'what was he doing here in the first place?'

'Why would an ordinary burglar want to ruin the pictures like that?' the woman cleaner said. 'It'd be a waste of time.'

Miss Frayle swung round as Hugo Coltman and the other woman cleaner came through the door from the old house.

Miss Frayle hurried to him. 'It's Dicky Bennett,' she said.

Coltman made no reply. She followed after him as he went quickly to the stage. He looked down then knelt beside Dicky

Bennett. He felt the boy's pulse, and touched the head to look at the wound from which the blood had come. 'The doctor should be here any moment.' Then he said: 'Whatever was he doing here at all?'

'You'll be able to find that out,' Miss Frayle said, 'when he recovers consciousness.'

Hugo Coltman nodded; and then a tubby little man appeared, to join them on the stage. His words brought a chill to Miss Frayle's heart. 'Concussion,' he said. 'It may be some time before he comes out of this.'

'Was it an accident?' Miss Frayle said.

Dr. Hewitt looked up at her in some astonishment. 'Unless somebody struck him a blow with some blunt instrument,' he said. 'But that's not likely, is it?'

'Of course not,' Hugo Coltman said, his eyes flashing a warning to Miss Frayle. 'On the face of it, he fell from the stage and struck his head. It was an accident, undoubtedly.'

Miss Frayle decided that this was not the moment to blurt out the facts of the damage to the paintings. She glanced at Baxter and the women cleaners and shook her head meaningly. It was obvious that Hugo Coltman would not want the news spread around about the paintings.

'I'll phone for the ambulance,' Dr. Hewitt said.

'I will take you to my office,' Coltman said.

'And Bennett's parents should know what's happened,' Miss Frayle said. 'They'll have missed him by now, and they must be terribly worried.'

'Telephone them at once,' Hugo Coltman said. 'Perhaps they can throw some light on what he was doing here, anyway. He had no right to be here, none at all.'

He swung away, and it was then that he saw the picture transfixed by the sword. He stepped forward towards the footlights and his gaze ranged over the other slashed canvases.

'My portraits.' And now Coltman was galvanized into action. He shot down the steps from the stage and into the auditorium, a strange sound coming from his throat. Miss Frayle awaited the outburst of anger. Coltman's face had paled to dead white, his mouth hung open and quivered. In cold fury he walked forward, and his hands went to his head in despair as he glared at the destroyed paintings.

Miss Frayle, Baxter, and the others stood there in a frozen tableau, holding their breath. Finally Coltman spoke, forming the words with difficulty, to Baxter:

'Take them down. Have them carried to my study.'

'I'm sure it wasn't Dicky Bennett,' Miss Frayle said. 'It couldn't have been him.'

Her voice trailed off as Coltman ignored her; his whole being seemed to be concentrated on the pictures. He watched as Baxter moved towards the paintings, then hesitated. 'Should we touch them, sir? I mean — '

'Or the sword?' Miss Frayle said. 'There might be fingerprints. The police — '

She jumped back, startled, as he rounded on her, blazing with sudden fury, his face mottled, the veins on his forehead swelling.

'What in hell are you talking about, Miss Frayle? This is a private matter. I'll handle it in my own way. The police have no concern here. None at all. If some maniac chooses to make these dastardly attacks on me, it's my affair, and I shall find the culprit.' He turned back to Baxter. 'Do as I say, take these paintings down.'

He strode through the auditorium and through the door to the old house, leaving Miss Frayle agape at his violent reaction, Dr. Hewitt and Baxter, the latter standing sullenly, with hunched shoulders, looking after him. 'He won't be able to keep the police out of this,' Baxter said to Miss Frayle. 'What are the boy's parents going to say for a start, when they know?'

Some half-hour later, after the ambulance had taken young Bennett, followed by the doctor, to hospital, Miss Frayle found Hugo Coltman in his office. He was sitting quietly at his desk, upon which, neatly arrayed, were two or three photographs of actors, suitably inscribed. More photographs of actors and actresses adorned the walls, and there were old theatre programmes and pictures of the old-time theatrical stars.

'Sit down, Miss Frayle,' Hugo Coltman said. 'I wished to apologize for my behaviour in the theatre this morning.'

'That's all right,' she said brightly. 'I can understand how you felt.'

'I suffered not inconsiderable shock, and indeed, horror, at the treatment of my portraits.' He indicated the canvases, which now leaned in one corner of the room.

Miss Frayle's horn-rims travelled from them to the framed photographs of Coltman in his stage rôles, which took up a lot of the wall-space directly behind his magnificent head, pictures of him standing arrogant and a trifle self-satisfied in the centre of groups of actors and actresses who had appeared with him in his productions.

The windows opened on to a lawn with flowering shrubs and trees. A pleasant room, fit setting for the sometimes flamboyant personality of the man who had brought to life and built up the Hugo Coltman Drama Workshop.

Now Coltman sat broodingly, staring at the sword which rested glittering on his desk. He touched it with distaste.

'Who wielded this?' he said suddenly. 'Tell me, Miss Frayle, was it that young idiot Bennett, or some unknown, the same unknown, who caused his injuries?'

'If we had been able to get it checked for fingerprints,' she said hesitantly, but he interrupted her.

'That is what I wanted to discuss with you. I insist that there must be no question of calling in the police. That would mean publicity — the wrong kind of publicity.'

'But when Bennett recovers,' Miss Frayle said, 'and if he says somebody did attack him?'

Coltman's eyes held hers as he cut in harshly:

'That chance must be taken. Meanwhile we will attempt to discover the culprit ourselves, without outside assistance.' He hesitated. 'Don't you see, Miss Frayle, for my students to panic and leave would mean disaster for me,' he went on. 'I wish you to understand this plainly.

There must not be a hint of danger to the students.'

He paused, while Miss Frayle watched him draw a finger along the sword-blade up to the hilt. Then he seemed to realize what he was doing and again he assumed an expression of distaste, and his fingers drummed on the desk.

'Whether Bennett met his injuries accidentally,' he said, 'or whether they were inflicted by somebody else, the fact remains that he had no right, absolutely no right, to be prowling around the theatre at night. I shall see that the other students are protected. If this unknown maniac aims further blows at me in his malice — '

'You mean,' Miss Frayle said, 'you don't think it is Dicky Bennett or one of the students?'

'I don't know,' Coltman paused reflectively: 'Bennett may be a young fool, but I cannot believe he is vicious enough to have slashed those paintings, to have driven the sword into the portrait of myself in such a symbolic manner. That, Miss Frayle, shows a diseased mind.' He stood up and paced up and down slowly.

'Whatever brought him to the theatre?' Miss Frayle said. 'I think he must have come across the person who did do it, perhaps surprised him in the act.'

'Possibly,' Hugo Coltman said. 'But as I have made plain to you, Miss Frayle, I cannot afford to risk any further incidents. We must act with the utmost discretion if I am not to be ruined.'

Miss Frayle spoke suddenly and boldly, voicing an idea that had lain at the back of her mind even before she arrived in the study.

'You don't want the police brought in,' she said, 'and I understand that, of course. But there's someone else who would act with great discretion, and who would solve this mystery if anybody can.'

He glanced at her inquiringly. 'Who might that be, Miss Frayle?'

'Dr. Morelle,' she said.

10

In the common-room there was a buzz of conversation. Jeff Sullivan lounged in an armchair smoking a pipe. Roy Allen sat by the window staring moodily into space, his strong spatulate fingers entwined. Elspeth Finch, who had just arrived from the town, was chatting with Theodore Willard, while she threw oblique glances at Allen.

Jeff Sullivan smiled and got to his feet as Isobel Ross came into the room. 'Morning, Isobel,' he said, through a cloud of tobacco-smoke. 'You look very fresh and bright this morning. Considering what's happened.'

'I was up early and have been out for a walk,' Isobel said, her green eyes sparkling. 'Considering what?'

The others looked at her, and Jeff showed surprise.

'Haven't you heard? Young Bennett got knocked out in the theatre last night.'

'Bennett,' she said. 'How? What happened?'

Sullivan shrugged. 'He fell from the roof; he tripped over his own shadow; he was stabbed in the back; he was struck on the head. He's badly injured, slightly hurt, dead; murdered — you pays your penny and takes your choice.'

'I don't think there's anything to be funny about,' Willard said.

Sullivan looked at him. Elspeth Finch had turned abruptly away from Willard, who, left on his own, had moved towards Sullivan and Isobel Ross. There was an odd light in his eyes, and Sullivan wondered if it was on account of something the Finch woman had said to him.

'I'm not being funny,' he said. He turned back to Isobel. 'The whole place is in a flap. Apparently the cleaners found him early this morning.'

'But what was he doing in the school last night at all?' Isobel said.

'No idea,' Jeff said.

Theodore Willard broke in again, his voice sharp and rasping.

'It seems that the Coltman picture gallery has been slashed to pieces.' Isobel stared at him. 'The pictures have been carted away, I looked in to see. The walls are bare. Baxter told me every one had been cut to ribbons. Some madman at work, if it wasn't Bennett.'

At that moment Miss Frayle came in, and everyone turned to her.

'Is it true?' Willard said. 'Is the boy alive or dead?'

Miss Frayle's hands fluttered. 'Alive, yes, but his skull's fractured.'

'Poor kid,' Isobel Ross said. 'But how could it have happened?'

'Nobody knows,' Miss Frayle said, 'and Bennett may not be able to tell us for some time.'

'But what was he doing there at all?' Roy Allen said. He had left the window and joined the others round Miss Frayle. 'He lives in the town; whatever was he up to, skulking around the theatre in the small hours?'

'Only Dicky Bennett can tell us that,' Miss Frayle said.

'If he was attacked by someone,' Isobel

Ross said, 'because he followed them into the theatre — '

'That's too fantastic,' Allen said. 'Who on earth would want to harm young Bennett?'

'Whoever it was who damaged Hugo's pictures might have had good reason for knocking him out,' Jeff Sullivan said bluntly. 'If the kid caught him at it.'

'In that case he'll be able to identify the intruder,' said Isobel.

'Perhaps,' Jeff said. 'If he recognized him in the dark.'

So the news about the paintings was getting around fast, Miss Frayle thought. Soon all the students would know and that meant all the town in no time.

'It was bright moonlight,' Isobel was saying. 'But what brought him out in the first place?'

'Perhaps,' said Miss Frayle thoughtfully, 'he had heard something, seen something.' She broke off and blinked at the others over her glasses. 'I mean, he might have discovered this person meant to do something else to upset Mr. Coltman.'

'Whoever slashed those pictures was the same idiot who went crazy the other afternoon,' Willard said, interrupting her. 'Obviously the same hand at work. The same insane maniac.'

'Those paintings,' Isobel said, 'they were the pride of Hugo's life. Whoever did that wasn't so crazy, just horribly malicious. He knew what he was doing, he knew he was hitting Hugo where it would hurt most.'

'It can't be anything like that,' Roy Allen said. 'More likely one of the students with his knife in Hugo and showing it, like a destructive child.'

Elspeth Finch's voice broke in, mockingly.

'For myself, I can't see why it mightn't have been Bennett himself. That seems the most likely explanation. After all, he did break into the place. He slashed the paintings, and then lost his footing in the darkness, and knocked himself out. Serve the little beast right.'

Isobel Ross swung on her, her eyes flashing. 'Dicky Bennett wouldn't do a thing like that. I know he's a bit scatterbrained, even reckless, but he's not vicious and revengeful.'

'All the same, it is more likely, if it is a student,' Roy Allen said, 'to be someone living outside the school. I mean a student sleeping here wouldn't be able to slip out of his dormitory so easily without being spotted.'

'That's true,' said Elspeth Finch, and she glanced at Isobel again. 'If it isn't Bennett, then, perhaps it's someone we'd never have suspected. Perhaps not Dicky Bennett, but one of the hard-working, brainy sort.'

Isobel ignored the insinuation in the other's remark. 'There's no reason to believe that any student harbours such hatred for Hugo,' she said. 'This — this joker,' she continued with a burst of anger, 'obviously hates him to the extent of bringing him and the Workshop into disrepute.'

Sullivan nodded. 'Yes, it's somebody with a pretty fierce grudge,' he said, and then grinned suddenly. 'Let's hope he doesn't start attacking the staff next. Better be careful, Elspeth. Keep on the right side of your lot, or you'll find one of them coming at you with a meat-axe.'

Miss Frayle felt certain she saw a flicker of alarm appear in Elspeth Finch's eyes for a moment. 'That's a horrible thing to say,' Elspeth Finch said, and she glanced at all of them. 'Hugo should call the police in.'

'He will surely?' Isobel said, and she turned to Miss Frayle, who started to flutter and look unhappily at them.

'Mr. Coltman's rather strongly opposed to — to outside intervention,' she said. 'He means to clear up the matter himself.'

'What?' Sullivan said, while Willard gave a snort of amazement.

'That's nonsense,' Isobel said sharply. 'How on earth can he expect to get to the bottom of something like this?'

'When something is liable to happen at any moment,' Roy Allen said. 'Something even worse.'

'I was thinking of that,' Isobel said.

There was a short silence. Miss Frayle found herself watching the play of emotion on the faces turned to her. There was still little real sympathy for Hugo Coltman in any of their expressions, she thought. There was hostility in them all, or was she merely imagining it? Then she asked herself: Was each one of them laughing secretly in the recesses of a malicious half-insane mind?

The door opened violently. Hugo Coltman strode in, as everyone started, nerves tingling. Gripped in his hand was the long gleaming sword Miss Frayle had last seen on his desk. Coltman stood there, looking straight at Jeff Sullivan. When he spoke his voice, though harsh and bitter, was well controlled.

'I think you can tell me something about this sword?'

There was a moment of electric silence. Miss Frayle and everybody else stared at Jeff Sullivan. He faced Coltman's accusing figure, and after the first surprise his manner was easy and calm, even mocking. He said in a pleasant drawl:

'If I may look more closely at it?' He bent to examine it. 'Yes, I can tell you something about it. It belongs to me.'

'But, Jeff,' Isobel Ross said, 'it's not one

of your fencing-foils. They have buttons at the point. This is sharp.' She shuddered a little, as Coltman raised the blade dramatically, so that all could see the sharpened point of the sword.

'It belongs to me all right,' Sullivan said. 'It's one of a pair of old Spanish rapiers that I picked up in Cadiz, as a matter of fact. It is of fine Toledo steel, and is pretty valuable.'

He smiled quizzically at Coltman, whose expression did not soften.

'I wondered,' Coltman said, 'if you can explain how it came to be used to slash my pictures in the theatre, finally to be plunged viciously into a portrait of myself in the rôle of King Lear?'

Jeff Sullivan took it coolly. He shrugged.

'I can't explain that. I have no idea how it happened.'

'But you are the one who might be expected to know. You knew where it was kept.'

'So did plenty of other people,' Sullivan said. 'They are always kept in a cupboard in the gymnasium. Plenty of people know that. If you're accusing me — ' He broke off, smiling thinly. 'How do you know you didn't do it yourself, walking in your sleep?'

'This is not the moment for comments of that nature,' Coltman said.

'Why don't you get the police to find out?' Roy Allen said.

Coltman swung on him. 'The police will not enter into this,' he said shortly. It was plain to Miss Frayle that he was discomfited by Sullivan's cool reaction to his veiled insinuations. For one wild moment she wondered if Sullivan had hit upon the true explanation of what had happened in the theatre. Could it have been Hugo Coltman walking in his sleep? Then she caught her breath as, still bland and smiling, Sullivan said:

'The onus of proof is on the prosecution, you know.' His tone was light and casual as he went on. 'The accused man is presumed innocent until proved otherwise.'

For a moment Hugo Coltman seemed to swell up. Miss Frayle saw the danger signs of the protruding veins on his temples. Then with a visible effort he controlled himself. He seemed to realize Sullivan had completely taken the wind out of his sails, his arrogance collapsed. With one of his swift changes of mood, the controlled emotions of the skilled actor, he said quietly:

'Would you mind, Mr. Sullivan, if I keep this for the moment?'

'By all means keep it,' Jeff shrugged, adding, with a glint in his eyes: 'I shan't ask you for a receipt for it.'

Hugo Coltman switched to an attitude of slightly offended dignity. His gaze swept the others.

Theodore Willard smirked openly. Miss Frayle had observed him enjoying the exchanges between Sullivan and Coltman and revelling in the latter's discomfiture. Breathing hard, Hugo Coltman looked round at them all again, with a bitter twist to his mobile mouth. 'I intend,' he said, 'to get to the heart of this mystery.'

He turned on his heel and made a dramatic exit, giving no sign that he had suffered any defeat. A silence followed his departure. Then Willard spoke.

'Either he thinks Bennett slashed his

pictures,' he said, 'and then knocked himself out accidentally, or he now suspects all of us.' He swung upon Jeff Sullivan. 'He suspects you, because you own the sword. He suspects me because he knows I resent his arrogant bombast. He suspects you, Roy, because — '

'Why should he suspect me?' Roy Allen said, with unusual violence. 'I've done nothing to him. All I want is to be allowed to carry on with my music in peace.'

'Does he suspect me, Theodore,' Elspeth Finch said, 'because I speak my mind too freely?'

'And how about me?' said Isobel sweetly, and Miss Frayle saw her dislike of Willard showing in her eyes. 'Why does he suspect me?'

Willard shrugged. 'You know the answer to that better than I,' he said. He moved to the door. 'I suppose work must go on.' With a sneer spreading across his face, he said:

'Let Hugo C. himself do what he may,
The cat will mew and dog will have his day.'

They all began moving after him. In the hall, Miss Frayle paused, tyres were crunching on the gravel drive, and through the open door she saw a saloon car pull up outside.

A comfortably plump man in a sober business suit got out, and opened the door for a middle-aged woman. He was gentle and attentive, and Miss Frayle guessed at once who they were. The Bennetts, Dicky's parents. Her hands fluttering, she met them at the doorway. 'Mr. and Mrs. Bennett?'

'Yes, we are,' the man said. There was a business-like no-nonsense air about him, and Miss Frayle could not help feeling he was not the sort who would be put off by Coltman.

'I'm Miss Frayle,' she said. 'Mr. Coltman's secretary.'

'Thank you for ringing us up,' Mrs. Bennett said. Miss Frayle caught the quaver in her voice. 'We've just come from the hospital.'

'I'm so sorry about it,' Miss Frayle said. 'It's an awful business.'

'He's still unconscious,' the man said.

'They said it might be some time before he comes round. There's nothing we can do but wait.'

'What's so horrible,' Mrs. Bennett said, 'is the idea of someone attacking him, Dicky would never harm anyone.'

'We don't know yet whether he was attacked,' Miss Frayle said hastily. 'It may have been an accidental fall, you see.'

'We'll get to the bottom of it — or the police will,' Bennett said, and Miss Frayle halted as she led them into the hall, her heart sinking. 'This matter's got to be cleared up properly,' the man was continuing. 'Dicky was telling us about some stupid goings-on here. Now he's become the victim of this business. If there's a lunatic here, he'd better be found and double quick. I'm going to insist on it. We have every right, as Dicky's parents.'

'Of course. Naturally,' Miss Frayle said, flustered. 'If you'll just wait in my office, I'll tell Mr. Coltman you're here.'

She went through and found Hugo Coltman glowering at the sword, which still rested on his desk. 'Dicky Bennett's parents are here.'

He stood up, and straightened his shoulders, and, fascinated, Miss Frayle saw him change magically from an embittered, suspicious individual into the sort of genial, expansive man in whom all parents could put their trust. Hugo Coltman, as so often before, was deliberately putting on an act. He came forward with hand extended as Miss Frayle led the Bennetts into his study. His expression was a mixture of friendliness and sympathy. His voice was firm, with undertones of kindly solicitude.

'So glad to see you both,' he said. 'So deeply distressed at this unfortunate occurrence.'

Miss Frayle stood by the door, as Coltman's voice became more persuasive, at its most mellifluous.

'The point is, what's going to be done about it,' Bennett said bluntly.

Hugo Coltman's fine eyebrows rose. 'My dear Mr. Bennett, everything possible will be done for your son. I understand from Dr. Hewitt to whom I spoke just now — '

'I mean, find out how it happened,' Bennett said.

Miss Frayle threw Hugo Coltman an agitated look, but he remained calm. 'Let us get this unfortunate occurrence in its proper perspective,' he said. 'After all, it has really arisen from a childish, practical joke — '

'Practical joke?' Bennett said, and there was an edge to his voice, so that Mrs. Bennett looked at him as if apprehensive that he was angry. 'It's a poor sort of joke when my son gets badly injured. Who did it, that's what I want to know?'

Coltman spread his hands. 'We do not know that anyone did anything. Unless Dicky, on recovery, tells us that he was in fact attacked by someone.'

'But he must have been attacked,' Mrs. Bennett said.

'I'm sorry, but I cannot agree with you, I would say that the circumstances point strongly to an accidental fall.'

'Then call the police in, and let them find out,' said Bennett.

'I think you may safely leave the decision whether to invite the police to investigate the matter, or not, to me,' Coltman said, his tone calm and controlled. As Mr. Bennett started to speak he leaned forward across his desk and said: 'Has it not occurred to you to wonder what your son was doing in the theatre at all at that time of night, when he should, one would imagine, have been home in bed?'

'I know,' Bennett said, less confidently, 'that's something we can't understand ourselves. But that — '

'May I say something?' Coltman said, and without giving the other a chance to reply, he went on: 'I've no wish to upset you at this time, but the fact remains that your son had no right to be where he was when he suffered his injury in the theatre. He had, in fact, broken into the building.'

A stifled gasp from Mrs. Bennett interrupted him, but only briefly. He went on, after a kindly glance at her: 'You see? We know of no earthly reason why he should have been there. Some boyish prank? Who can say? But if the police were brought in his boyish prank might very well be regarded as in a more, shall we say, unkind light. Do you really wish him to be lying there with police by his bedside waiting to question him?'

'No, of course not,' Mrs. Bennett said. 'Of course we don't want further trouble for Dicky.'

Hugo Coltman turned to Bennett who was pursing his lips. He turned back to the woman. 'So glad you see my point of view, Mrs. Bennett. And I do suggest, for the time being, that we keep this business between ourselves. Then, when your son is recovered, and can tell us what really happened, you can rely on me to act accordingly, always with the knowledge that I should act only in his and your best interests.'

They went, the man a trifle chastened, his wife with a trusting smile at Hugo Coltman. Miss Frayle waited for him to return after showing them out. She heard the sound of the car receding and then he came back into his study. He seemed to collapse into his chair, and his shining eyes now lacked lustre. He looked harassed, uncertain once more.

'You were marvellous with them,' she said.

He shook his head and glanced up at her with a haggard look. 'If only I could feel convinced that those people won't decide after all to go chattering to the police.' His head sank on his chest. 'If only — ' He broke off and looked at her. 'I really think I should take your advice, Miss Frayle,' he said.

11

It was about half an hour later, and Miss Frayle, her step jaunty, her eyes very bright behind her horn-rims, hurried out of her office next to Hugo Coltman's study, and encountered Isobel Ross.

'I was just coming to see you,' Isobel said. 'Any news of Dicky Bennett?'

'None, so far,' Miss Frayle said. She added brightly: 'But at any rate Dr. Morelle is coming down to investigate the whole business.' Even as she said it, she realized she had been indiscreet. She ought not to have mentioned it to anyone. Dr. Morelle would be furious with her for having said anything at all about his arrival on the scene. She groaned inwardly.

Isobel Ross's eyebrows rose. 'Dr. Morelle? That means dear Hugo must have climbed down a little.'

'Perhaps I shouldn't have mentioned it,' Miss Frayle said hurriedly. 'You won't tell anyone else, will you? It's all going to be handled very quietly, and discreetly.'

'I won't breathe a word,' Isobel said. She was glancing over Miss Frayle's shoulder, and Miss Frayle turned to see Brian Wickham coming towards them. She was struck by his pallor, and his eyes were unnaturally bright.

'Miss Ross, can I speak to you?' he said jerkily. 'My head's all muzzy, and — ' He broke off, his mouth quivering. 'I'm so worried — about Dicky.'

Miss Frayle thought that he looked dangerously near a nervous breakdown.

'Dicky Bennett?' Isobel said.

'I feel terrible about what happened,' Wickham went on. 'You see it's all my fault — '

'Your fault?' Isobel Ross said, sharply. 'What could you have had to do with it?'

'I didn't mean I had anything to do with his getting hurt,' the other said. 'It's only that I was worried by what happened the other day — you know,' he turned to Miss Frayle, 'when Dr. Morelle was here. And Dicky had this idea that there was going to be more trouble.'

'Why?' Miss Frayle said. 'Why was he afraid something else could happen?'

'I don't really know,' Wickham said. 'It — it was just a feeling he had, and I — I sort of encouraged him. If I'd had any sense at all I'd have told him to lay off the whole thing.'

'Yes,' Isobel Ross said impatiently, 'but why did you say it was your fault that Dicky was injured?'

'It was because of this idea we had. You see, we decided it would be a good idea if Dicky and I and one or two others kept watch for anything that might point to the person who'd played those tricks — '

'Did you find out anything?' Isobel Ross said.

'I don't know if Dicky tumbled on something. But I think he must have decided to come in last night and see if everything was all right.'

'So that's why he was here,' Miss Frayle said. She saw that Isobel Ross was looking her way warningly. What Wickham had just said might imply that young Bennett had in fact been attacked by someone,

someone whom the student had disturbed in the theatre. As Miss Frayle fell silent, a dozen conjectures spinning round in her mind, Isobel Ross had turned to Wickham.

'But,' she said, 'how could he have got into the place so easily? It was locked up.'

'There's a wonky window-catch in the gym,' Wickham said.

Then, Miss Frayle thought, if he and young Bennett knew about that, anybody besides them could have known about it and got in the same way.

'Don't you see?' Brian Wickham said. 'It's really my fault Dicky was hurt. If I hadn't let him go ahead with the whole idea.'

'You've nothing to reproach yourself with,' Isobel Ross said. 'It was as much Bennett's enthusiasm. He looked upon it as an exciting adventure. Forget it. No point in upsetting yourself.'

'Dicky will be all right,' Miss Frayle said soothingly.

'I'm sorry,' Brian Wickham said. 'I shouldn't have bothered you. Thank you, Miss Ross — and you, Miss Frayle.'

He turned and walked away with nervous jerky steps. Miss Frayle watched him go along the hall, uneasily.

Isobel Ross said thoughtfully: 'Rotten luck that he's concerned with this. His whole future depends upon the next week. He's the nervy type, and I have high hopes for him — if he doesn't go to pieces.' Miss Frayle murmured sympathetically. 'What a business,' Isobel said. 'Anyway, let's hope young Bennett can help when he comes round.'

Miss Frayle nodded, and then it occurred to her that it must be a nasty feeling for whoever had attacked Dicky Bennett, if anybody had, wondering whether their identity would be given away within a few hours. She pushed her horn-rims back into place; with a sudden shock she realized something else: if Dicky Bennett had been in danger in the theatre might he not yet be in danger still? Say this shadowy assailant somehow got into the hospital and silenced him before he could speak?

She left Isobel Ross, who returned to her class, and made her way in search of

Coltman to inform him that she had telephoned Dr. Morelle and had persuaded him to come down to the Coltman Drama Workshop that afternoon. She had arranged accommodation for him at the best local hotel.

She found Hugo Coltman taking one of his own classes in the theatre, and she managed to draw him aside for a moment to give him her news. He replied monosyllabically, his attention upon the class of students, and she went off to return to her office.

Over her lunch, which she had early in the dining-room, her thoughts turned to the encounter in the hall with Isobel Ross, and then young Wickham joining in. What a strange, distraught state he was in, she thought. Was his agitation really due to his concern for Dicky Bennett? Or was it because of something he had done and for which he himself felt guilty? Was it he who was in fact responsible for all that had shaken the calm of the Drama Workshop these past few days, even to the extent of harming his own cousin in some crazed fury?

It was another piece to the jigsaw which was scattered in her head as she entered her office.

As she went in she caught a slight sound beyond the half-open door of the study. She thought it might be Coltman himself there and she went in, then halted on the threshold.

Elspeth Finch was there, alone. She was intently studying the photographs massed on the wall above Coltman's desk. Miss Frayle saw an enigmatic smile on her face. She swung round as Miss Frayle stood there and the odd smile had not completely gone. There was a faraway look in her dark eyes, and Miss Frayle sensed an air of excitement about her.

'I thought it was Mr. Coltman,' Miss Frayle began, but the other interrupted her coolly.

'I came to have a talk with him,' she said. 'As he wasn't here, I thought I'd wait.'

She made a slim, oddly graceful figure as she nodded her dark, sleek head towards the photographs, and smiled again, faintly.

'It's the first time I've really looked at them, although I've been in the room before, of course. Between ourselves, I see quite enough of Hugo in the flesh.' There was an acid tone in her voice. 'The past career of the great Hugo — all in pictures. Really they arouse some thoughts.'

'What d'you mean?' Miss Frayle moved to the photographs, peering through her glasses at them.

The one which Elspeth Finch appeared to have been studying was Hugo Coltman and a group of players in costume. One man alone, at the end of the row, wore ordinary clothes.

'Just a theory,' Elspeth Finch said, after a pause. She nodded at the photograph. ''School For Scandal' — appropriate, don't you think, considering what's going on here now?'

What on earth did the woman mean? Miss Frayle thought that there was a knowing air about those glittering eyes, that hard tight smile.

Then Miss Frayle glanced at the clock on the desk, and all speculation was driven from her mind. It was approaching two-thirty. Dr. Morelle was due at his hotel in half an hour and she had assured him she would be there to welcome him and over a quiet cup of tea acquaint him with all that had transpired since the afternoon of his visit. She gave Elspeth Finch a fluttering smile. Elspeth did not return her smile and Miss Frayle hesitated and then went out, a vague feeling of anxiety clouding her mind.

Elspeth Finch stood for several minutes after Miss Frayle had gone. Then, quickly and deftly, as if she might have rehearsed it, she took down the 'School For Scandal' photograph. With slightly trembling fingers, she slipped the picture from its frame, and folding it in half, slid it underneath her jacket, where it could not be seen.

She hesitated again for a moment, the frame in her hand. Then she took down another picture, half hidden in the shadows of a corner of the room, and hung it in the place of the one she had taken.

The empty frame she put in the corner. Half obscured with the light shining across the glass, it was difficult for a casual observer to see that it contained no photograph.

Elspeth Finch hurried from the room, swift and silent, the same enigmatic smile touching her mouth.

12

Dr. Morelle's yellow Duesenberg drew up outside the Lamb and Flag, and Miss Frayle, who had arrived a few minutes earlier, hurried out to him. Asking her temporarily to restrain her torrent of news, he stalked into the hotel and arranged for his suitcase to be taken up to his room. Then he found a corner of the quiet, comfortable lounge and ordered tea.

'Now, Miss Frayle, release the flood-gates.'

Miss Frayle, who had been fighting a battle with herself in the effort to control her impatience, plunged forthwith into a detailed account of the happenings of the past four days at Hugo Coltman's Drama Workshop.

Eyes half closed against the smoke curling up from his inevitable Le Sphinx, Dr. Morelle listened.

Over the telephone Miss Frayle had

given him a brief outline of the sinister events of the dramatic academy, culminating in the discovery early that morning of Dicky Bennett's unconscious figure in the theatre. What Miss Frayle had told him had been enough to convince Dr. Morelle that Coltman's invitation to him to investigate the matter was sufficiently compelling for him to accept it.

He had, of course, been careful to let no hint fall to Miss Frayle of his own ulterior motive in taking this opportunity to come down to the house again. Watching Miss Frayle now she was, he imagined, blissfully unaware of what lay at the back of his mind concerning her. She could not suspect what life at 221b Harley Street had been like for him the past week, work becoming more and more impossible, very soon it would be chaos. Gone were the days when every hour had moved along smoothly and to plan, when his notes and papers were neatly filed and indexed. Of course he had been forced to accept certain irritations about Miss Frayle which had jarred his sensibilities at times. But that was a price he was prepared to pay.

'There appears to be no proof yet,' he observed presently, 'from what you have said, that if Bennett was attacked, the assailant was not someone other than Coltman's students, or a member of his staff.'

'Even if you don't think this is anything to do with any student,' Miss Frayle said. 'I don't see how it could be anyone outside.'

'What you say may be right,' Dr. Morelle said through a cloud of cigarette-smoke, 'which leads inevitably to the suspicion that the culprit is one of the teachers.'

'They're all pretty much on edge with one another,' Miss Frayle said. 'And what's more they're critical of Mr. Coltman, their attitude seems to have built up the last week or two. The whole atmosphere is not what you'd call happy at all, it's as if a sense of doom or disaster is being deliberately generated by someone.'

'The man Sullivan seems a reckless and adventurous type,' Dr. Morelle said, musingly. 'While the two others, Willard and Allen, might appear to possess somewhat neurotic tendencies. Though one must not judge any of them too hastily. Allen, for instance, a composer whose mind is filled with music in a half-formed stage might tend to appear absent-minded and vague.' He paused then went on. 'Assuming Bennett was attacked, some strength on the part of his assailant might have been involved. Would you say that one of them is more likely to be predisposed to violence?'

'I don't know,' Miss Frayle said. 'Perhaps Sullivan is a tougher sort. But come to that, Isobel Ross is, for instance, a strong well-built woman. As capable as any man of being able to attack a young boy. Or Elspeth Finch, she's got a frightful temper.'

Dr. Morelle smiled at her. 'I see,' he said, 'you have retained those powers of observation, which, if I may say so, I perhaps helped inspire in you, when we were — er — working together.'

Miss Frayle blushed suitably. And then Dr. Morelle was stubbing out his cigarette while she gulped back the rest of her cup of tea and she was following him out of the hotel. The Duesenberg revved into life and they were heading out of the town.

Hugo Coltman greeted Dr. Morelle with a restrained air of tragedy, plus a long-suffering manner.

'I am entirely at your disposal,' he said, 'as is the entire Workshop, its staff, or any of the students you may wish to talk to.'

'I would like to look at the theatre first,' Dr. Morelle said.

Hugo Coltman led the way and Miss Frayle followed them as he and Dr. Morelle went into the theatre. Dr. Morelle stood eyeing the place where Dicky Bennett had been discovered. Then he produced a magnifying-glass which he unfolded and examined the edge of the piano in the orchestra-pit. After a careful scrutiny, moving the magnifying-glass along the piano-edge he paused. 'This edge here,' he said, 'shows slight traces of blood, and hair.'

Miss Frayle gave a little gasp. Hugo Coltman took a step forward; he stared at the spot over which Dr. Morelle held the magnifying-glass.

'That means he struck his head there?' Coltman said. 'He fell from the stage?'

'Most probably that was what occurred,' Dr. Morelle said. 'That still does not answer the question — was his fall accidental?' He turned away. 'I should like to see the paintings that were slashed.'

Coltman led the way back to the study, and Dr. Morelle was bending over the ruined canvases.

'I admit I was intensely proud of them,' Hugo Coltman was saying, his voice trembling slightly. 'They would have done something to perpetuate my not unsuccessful career. I had thought of leaving to the — er — however, perhaps that sounds vainglorious on my part you may think. But I should have liked to have left something behind.'

For a moment Miss Frayle wondered if he was possessed by some premonition that his end was near, and a chill gripped her heart. She glanced at Dr. Morelle but his expression was enigmatic. After a few moments' contemplation of the slashed paintings, he said: 'I think I would like to see Dr. Hewitt. He may be able to throw further light on the boy's injuries.'

In the car on the way to the doctor's house, which was on the outskirts of the town, Dr. Morelle was thoughtful and Miss Frayle did not disturb his mood. Dr. Hewitt greeted Dr. Morelle warmly; it was obvious that his reputation was familiar to the other.

'I was just about to leave for the hospital, Dr. Morelle,' he said. 'Perhaps you'd like to come along with me.'

The three of them got into Dr. Morelle's car and on the way Dr. Hewitt described the condition in which he had found Dicky Bennett, and the nature of the injury he had suffered. He agreed with Dr. Morelle that the wound on his head was consistent with his having struck his head against the corner of the piano.

Dicky Bennett was in a small private ward. Miss Frayle, at Dr. Morelle's shoulder, looked down at the bandaged head. His eyelids were closed on waxy cheeks, his breathing was irregular.

A youngish fair-haired house-surgeon said: 'X-rays show there is a small piece of bone pressing on the brain. It has been decided to operate this evening.'

'Has he shown any signs of consciousness at all?' Dr. Morelle said.

The house-surgeon was about to answer when there was a slight movement from the bandaged figure, and a faint moan from the pallid lips. The deep silence in the room was broken only by Miss Frayle's quick breathing as she, Dr. Morelle and the two others stared at the eyelids fluttering momentarily. Dr. Morelle leaned over the bed as in a faint voice Dicky Bennett said:

'Dark hands . . . my mouth . . . '

There was another moan and the eyelids were still again.

Silence followed. Dr. Morelle straightened himself, and glanced at the others.

Without anyone saying anything they all went out of the room. 'Odd, he should have spoken then,' the house-surgeon said. 'Though it didn't make much sense.'

'It made a little sense,' Dr. Morelle said, and Miss Frayle experienced a tingle of excitement down her spine as she glanced at him. They left the house-surgeon in conversation with the nurse on duty as Miss Frayle, silent, tip-tapped along the polished corridors behind the gaunt, striding figure of Dr. Morelle and the bustling Dr. Hewitt.

After he had returned Dr. Hewitt to his house to prepare for his evening surgery, Dr. Morelle headed the Duesenberg back to the Lamb and Flag.

Dr. Morelle was silent before the wheel as the garish-hued, rakish-built car throbbed through the late afternoon sunlight. Miss Frayle looked at the lean hawk-like profile beside her. It was quite like old times, she was thinking, and a glow of happiness stole over her. Just like the old days it was.

True, this business at the Drama School, though it was upsetting and with undertones of something sinister, was not to be compared with some of the dark and macabre cases on which she had accompanied her former employer in the past, but she was out with Dr. Morelle on a case once more.

'We didn't learn very much from that poor boy, I'm afraid,' she said. 'Did we?'

The profile did not shift its attention from the road. Miss Frayle thought that Dr. Morelle had not heard what she had said, so absorbed had he been with his own thoughts.

'On the contrary,' the profile said, from the corner of its mouth, just as she was about once more to put what she had said to him, 'we learned quite a lot. We learned that Bennett was attacked, quite definitely, and that his assailant wore gloves. That would be the explanation of the phrase: dark hands.' He turned to her and she saw that his mouth had tightened. 'No doubt it's occurred to you, Miss Frayle, that if this unknown assailant's victim should die, this case would assume somewhat more serious aspects.'

'You mean — murder?'

'Precisely,' Dr. Morelle said. 'Murder.'

13

This evening, in the common-room, Elspeth Finch had flung herself into a chair, saying how tired she was, she could not go home until she'd had a rest. Jeff Sullivan, Theodore Willard, Isobel Ross and Roy Allen were there, reading or sitting idly, chatting.

'I suppose he was just the same then, arrogant and self-centred?' Elspeth Finch said. Willard had been telling her and Sullivan tales of Hugo Coltman when he had been a London star, drawing packed houses in Shaftesbury Avenue. Jeff Sullivan, lounging against the window, in a cloud of pipe smoke, grinned across at them.

'Worse, you bet,' he said. 'Now he's only got a few of us, then he had crowds of actors and everybody else to bully.'

'Everyone hated him,' Theodore Willard said. He turned to Roy Allen, but the latter seemed not to be listening. He sat brooding in a corner, making notes on a sheet of paper. Willard turned back to Isobel Ross, 'But there was one poor chap who had more reason to than anyone else,' he went on. 'At least so the story goes.'

'Who was that?' Elspeth Finch said.

'It was in the papers at the time,' Willard said. 'I was only reminded of it the other evening when I went up to the Old Vic and met an actor who'd been with Hugo in those days.'

'Don't leave us in suspense, Theo,' Elspeth said. 'Who hated our beloved employer more than anyone else?'

'It was a manager, named Wilson. A quiet sort of chap. It was when they were playing up North in a play which Hugo was bringing to London. According to what this chap was saying the other night, Wilson tried to pop off with the box-office takings.'

'I seem to remember hearing something about that,' Jeff Sullivan said. 'Hugo didn't let him get away with it, surely?'

Elspeth Finch had leant forward, 'Was he caught?'

Willard nodded. 'Got sent to prison.

Apparently a lot of people tried to get Hugo to do nothing. Said it would wreck the chap's career, and all that.'

'After all he did pinch the takings, you say,' Elspeth said with a sharp laugh. 'I don't see why he should expect to get away with that and no come-back.'

'Maybe,' Willard said. 'But plenty of people thought he might have been a bit more lenient. Wilson had been through a rough patch. He'd got a child who was ill and needed special treatment. According to this chap who was telling me about it, Wilson had everyone on his side, but Hugo wanted the man punished, and he got him a stretch.'

'I can just see dear Hugo in the witness-box,' Isobel Ross said. 'Giving his evidence as if he were playing King Lear.'

Elspeth Finch's sharp laugh again. 'Just his cup of tea,' she said. 'The blind goddess with the scales and sword. The letter of the law, and all humanity barred. He must have wallowed in all that.'

'Just now you were saying that the chap

deserved it,' Sullivan said, but the other shrugged.

'Who wouldn't be on anyone's side against Hugo,' she said.

Willard threw her a look, and Isobel Ross thought she caught a strange expression which she could not quite define at the back of his eyes. Then he turned to her as she asked him: 'What happened to him when he came out?'

'I don't know,' Willard said. 'The curtain was going up, and I didn't see the actor chap again.' He paused and then said: 'I seem to remember the play Hugo was doing at the time. 'School For Scandal', I believe it was.'

'I wonder,' Elspeth Finch said softly. Her dark eyes held a strange glint in them.

'You aren't linking that with the fun-and-games here, are you, Elspeth?' Isobel Ross said.

The other threw her a narrow glance. 'Good heavens, no,' she said. She jumped up from her chair. 'It was just that I was interested in Theo's gossip, that's all.' She gave them all an enigmatic look. Her gaze rested on Roy Allen, who was still scribbling absorbedly in the corner. He did not return her look, and she went out, humming to herself.

Jeff Sullivan eyed the door as it closed on her, and then looked at Isobel. He sniffed as if to say that Elspeth Finch was fathomless, then he spoke to Willard. 'What year did you say this was?'

'Not sure,' Willard said. 'But I think the chap said it was around 1935.'

Isobel glanced at him suddenly. 'I've got a vague idea I might have seen a picture of this man Wilson somewhere,' she said thoughtfully. 'Probably among those photos Hugo has in his study. I must have another look sometime.' She looked across at Roy Allen. 'How's your masterpiece shaping up, Roy?'

'Eh? What's that?' Roy Allen looked up absently.

'Your music,' she said. 'How are your tone-deaf young brats taking it?'

The other didn't smile, his face lit up with sudden enthusiasm. 'They're dead keen,' he said. 'There'll have been nothing like it for years, I can promise you.'

It was a tradition that the spring end-of-term show by the Drama Workshop students featured a musical or choral performance, this time it was to be a choral effort, for which Roy Allen was writing his special piece. Allen lit a cigarette, drew nervously at it, and sent a stream of smoke ceilingwards.

'Chant For Youthful Voices', isn't that what you're calling it?' Jeff Sullivan said. 'And,' he went on, 'is it true you're rehearsing two groups separately?'

Allen turned to glance at him. 'Yes, it's true. I'm training each lot on their own,' he said. 'The voice line and their own words, enough of the accompaniment to be sure of their entrance, but the whole thing won't finally be put together until the final performance. It — it's just an idea I have for it.'

'Taking a chance, isn't it?' Isobel said. 'How can you be sure they'll stick to their own parts when they hear other voices against them?'

Roy Allen stiffened slightly. Then he said easily: 'When I've finished with them they'll be able to sing it in their sleep.' He spread his hands. 'It may result in a less polished performance, but I particularly want that work to be heard for the first time at the end-of-term show.'

'It's your baby,' Jeff Sullivan said pleasantly, 'how it comes off is your business.'

Was there something remote and mysterious about Roy Allen's smile? For a moment Isobel Ross wondered, then it seemed to her his eyes wore a faraway look once more, as if he was listening in his mind to music, soaring away to the heights of his inspiration.

As Isobel turned to Jeff Sullivan, the door opened suddenly. Miss Frayle appeared on the threshold, Dr. Morelle behind her.

'You all met Dr. Morelle before, didn't you?' Miss Frayle said brightly. 'He — he's just looked in on Mr. Coltman again.'

Miss Frayle threw a quick glance at Isobel Ross who gave her an encouraging nod.

Dr. Morelle had followed her into the room. There was a murmur of conventional greetings from the others, except

Theodore Willard, who said with a meaning rasp in his voice: 'Just passing, Doctor, no doubt, and thought you'd drop in?'

Dr. Morelle turned a level gaze on him. 'I happened to be in this part of the world,' he said suavely.

'Any more news about young Bennett?' Isobel Ross said to Miss Frayle.

'Still unconscious, I'm afraid,' Miss Frayle said. She glanced swiftly at Dr. Morelle. His face was enigmatic. 'They're operating this evening. I'm sure he'll be all right.'

'You don't think that whoever knocked him out, is likely to be pinched for his murder?' It was Jeff Sullivan who asked the question, but he wasn't looking at Miss Frayle, he was staring straight at Dr. Morelle.

'You mean if anybody did attack him,' Willard said, 'and it wasn't just an accident?'

Miss Frayle sought Dr. Morelle's guidance in a brief, oblique glance. But he remained silent. 'It must have been an accident,' she said.

Isobel Ross looked at Dr. Morelle. 'There doesn't seem to be any clue that it was anything else but,' she said.

'I don't like it at all,' Willard said flatly. 'None of it. Whoever it is who's done these things, he — or she — it strikes me they're out of their minds. Don't you agree, Dr. Morelle, after all you yourself were a victim of some of the goings-on?'

'I would incline to the opinion,' Dr. Morelle said, 'that the culprit's actions may indicate some pathological tendency.'

Isobel Ross shivered. 'You make it sound quite creepy, Doctor,' she said.

'You may rest assured there is nothing supernatural, or creepy, about it,' Dr. Morelle said. He glanced at the others, then turned to Miss Frayle. 'I think I should like to say good night to Mr. Coltman before returning to my hotel.'

'Will you be staying long in these parts?' Jeff Sullivan said.

Dr. Morelle smiled a trifle thinly at him. 'That depends,' he said. He paused at the door and now his glance took in Miss Frayle. 'Though naturally,' he said, 'it has not been without considerable pleasure, meeting you all again, and I hope to improve upon our acquaintance.'

There was a murmur of good nights as he followed Miss Frayle out of the room.

Miss Frayle and Hugo Coltman saw the Duesenberg disappear out of sight through the drive-gates. Dr. Morelle would be calling again at the Drama Workshop in the morning, that was the arrangement arrived at.

Later that night Miss Frayle lay in bed, yet unable to sleep. Through the window of her room, which she had left open to the moonlit night, the curtains drawn back, came the small noises of the night. She heard a clock chiming midnight, and sighed. Her mind was far too active for sleep.

She sat up suddenly, her heart thudding. Was that a sound she had heard downstairs?

She listened, trying to still her rapid breathing, and switching on her bedside-lamp she found her glasses. There was no further sound. She must have been mistaken. Still tense, she lay back, then jerked up again.

She felt certain she could smell a faint, acrid smell. Smoke? Silently she swung out of bed, pushed her feet into her slippers and hurried into her dressing-gown.

For a moment she hesitated outside her door. The smell of burning was stronger. It was possible, she had thought, that a gardener had left a fire burning somewhere in the garden, and that the smoke of its smoulderings had drifted to her room. But now the burning smell seemed to her to be within the house.

She went quickly downstairs and instinctively ran silently to her office. She went in and stood there with a gasp. Through the open door to Hugo Coltman's study she saw the glare of fire, and smoke wreathing out towards her.

She rushed forward, and then, out of the corner of her eye, she glimpsed a movement behind the door. A violent blow caught her at the back of her head and she fell forward, sprawling over a waste-paper basket and crashing to the floor. Her glasses were flung away, and she lay there stunned.

A flame licked the wall, while the other smouldering tentacles reached across the floor towards where Miss Frayle lay.

14

There was a smashing of glass and the lower half of the study window slammed up. A gaunt, purposeful figure moved swiftly through into the room. Miss Frayle lay only two or three feet away from the leaping glare. Swiftly she was lifted and borne out through her office and into the hall.

As Dr. Morelle placed Miss Frayle down and saw her eyelids flutter and knew that she had come to no harm, other figures appeared in the hall aroused by the smashing of glass.

'Fire-extinguishers,' Dr. Morelle called out.

He hurried back into the study, Jeff Sullivan, who had quickly grabbed a fire-extinguisher from the hall, following him. Theodore Willard dashed off to fetch water. At that moment Hugo Coltman appeared, his quilted dressing-gown flowing behind him, his eyes staring as

Sullivan directed the spray from the fire-extinguisher on the blazing curtains.

'The fiend,' Coltman shouted. 'The fiend.'

Dr. Morelle's quick glance had seen that the fire had been started by papers heaped up in a corner. Photographs on the wall which the fire was attacking had crashed down in splintered glass and charred frames. The curtains were aflame, some of the furniture was scorched.

Now the extinguisher was doing good work, helped by buckets of water brought along by Willard, assisted by Isobel Ross and Roy Allen who had appeared on the scene, and Hugo Coltman himself. The fire was soon under control and subsiding. Any further damage was checked but the study was in a state of ruin.

'What insane idea is this?' Hugo Coltman was shouting. While he raged on, a wondering group stood there, in their nostrils the reek of charred paper, of scorched fabric and wood. Dr. Morelle had quitted the smoke-filled room to attend to Miss Frayle, who was recovering quickly from the attack upon her.

Isobel Ross came out to Miss Frayle, who was giving Dr. Morelle a hurried account of how she had come downstairs to investigate the smell of burning, and had been attacked. She had seen no one, she said, just a shadow moving quickly behind her, then the blow and blackness for her. There was a bump on the back of her head, but otherwise she had come to no harm.

Dr. Morelle handed her the horn-rims which he had picked up unbroken off the floor. 'I'll leave Miss Ross to help you back to your room,' he said. 'I want to have a look at the study for a few moments. I will see you in the morning.'

When he returned to the study he suggested to the others, that since there was nothing more to be done that night, they should return to bed. They went out, only Hugo Coltman was left with Dr. Morelle.

Coltman eyed him as he prowled around turning over the soaked debris, examining the wreckage that was all that remained of the photographs.

'Is there anything?' Coltman said, and

then he went on in a rush of words: 'When will this monster leave me alone? What lies behind it all? What have I done to deserve this of anyone?' He paused and then said: 'Why, Miss Frayle might have been burned to death. If you hadn't arrived when you did, she would have been.'

Dr. Morelle regarded him steadily. Coltman appeared to be on the brink of a nervous collapse.

'I promise you I will guide you out of this cloud of suspicion and hatred that has gathered round you,' Dr. Morelle said.

The other smiled at him wanly. He began to speak more calmly.

'Thank God you happened to be here,' he said. He gave Dr. Morelle a questioning look.

'I found it difficult to sleep,' Dr. Morelle said. 'And so I decided to take a stroll. Not unnaturally, since my waking thoughts were aimed at the mystery here, my footsteps led me in this direction. I found myself in the grounds,' Dr. Morelle continued, his face enigmatic, 'and was attracted by the glare of the flames. The rest you know.'

'You didn't see anyone leaving the place?'

'No,' Dr. Morelle said.

'Doesn't that prove it must have been someone inside?'

'Not proof. I imagine it wouldn't be difficult for someone who knew his — or her — way about to find a way in and out. It's a pretty rambling sort of house, and if it was an intruder from outside, a window-catch forced and the window left open for a quick exit, would provide no problem for someone as resourceful as this person appears to be.'

Hugo Coltman gazed bitterly round him. For the first time he noticed that Dr. Morelle carried something under his arm. 'Dr. Morelle, you've found something,' he said quickly.

Dr. Morelle smiled grimly, showed him a charred picture-frame, with the glass still intact.

'One of my photo-frames.'

'The remarkable thing about it being,' Dr. Morelle said, 'that it happens to be minus a photograph.'

Hugo Coltman's mouth fell open slightly as he took the photo-frame. Then he swung round at a movement in the doorway behind him.

'Elspeth Finch was looking at the photographs this afternoon.'

It was Miss Frayle who stood there, blinking at the empty photo-frame Coltman was holding. She could hardly repress her excitement as she blurted out: 'I found her in here.'

'I thought you had gone to bed,' Dr. Morelle said.

'I wanted to know what was happening down here,' she said.

Dr. Morelle's eyes had narrowed, and were glittering. He looked at Coltman whose expression was baffled. 'Miss Finch?' he said. 'Here, in my study? Was she interested in any particular photograph?'

'She said she was interested in them all,' Miss Frayle said. She decided she had better say nothing about Elspeth Finch's disparaging, sarcastic remarks concerning Hugo Coltman. 'But,' she went on, 'I do remember she was standing by one over there, now what was it? A stage group, I think it was 'School For Scandal'.'

Hugo Coltman took a step forward. 'Does that mean she removed the photograph out of the frame?' he said. 'And took it away?'

'It is possible,' Dr. Morelle said.

'And then you mean she started the fire to hide the theft?' Miss Frayle said.

Dr. Morelle shrugged non-committally. 'It may also mean,' he said, 'that whoever started the fire did not know that the photograph had been removed. The fire might have been started in an insane attempt,' he turned to Hugo Coltman, 'further to harass you and destroy the photographs you treasured. Or it could have been a calculated attempt to destroy one specific photograph.'

'Whichever way,' Coltman said, 'it doesn't seem that we're very much further ahead, does it?'

Dr. Morelle looked at him, his expression urbane and cool. 'Time has a way,' he said, 'of showing things in their true perspective. What appears to be a jumble of jigsaw pieces may soon fall neatly into place. Let us leave what at the moment we must to the future, and for the present return to sleep.' He turned to Coltman. 'Good night, and sleep without fear.'

'Sleep that knits up the ravell'd sleave of care,' Coltman said, and went out of the ruined study, his shoulders hunched disconsolately. Dr. Morelle stared after him for a moment, then his gaze flickered over Miss Frayle.

'Shall I show you to the door?' she said.

He nodded gravely. 'If you think it would be a more dignified exit for me than my entrance,' he said and followed her out.

15

Brian Wickham was sitting outside on the classroom window-sill, apart from several of the other students. It was approaching nine o'clock the next morning and the sunny air was sweet with the scent of early flowers. Reaching out absently, Wickham pulled one of the flowers towards him, fingering the petals. He could hear the voice of one of the students who was holding forth.

'I say something ought to be done. After all Dicky Bennett might've been killed. We ought to get the police in.' He turned to Wickham. 'Don't you think so, Brian?'

Wickham pretended not to hear, he tried to appear engrossed in his thoughts. The sense of guilt, of responsibility for Dicky's injury, had not left him, and now he had reached the stage when discussion of the incident was intolerable.

With an impatient movement he

snapped the flower stalk in his hand, and when he turned again the bloom was clutched in his fingers. One of the girl students who had turned to look at him whistled. 'Hey, don't let old Hugo see you pinching his precious pinks.'

She saw Wickham's tense face. She came over to him. 'You look pretty grim,' she said.

Wickham's smile was humourless. 'There's nothing the matter with me. Why should there be?'

'Why did you blackout yesterday?' she asked him bluntly. She was short and thick-set, with a boyish hair-cut and snubby face.

'It wasn't a blackout,' he said. 'I just dried up badly. I just couldn't remember, that's all. My mind went — it sort of went blank.'

Wickham dared not admit that the incident was more than just a temporary lapse. His memory had gone, leaving him helpless, bereft of the lines that had provided the solid background for his vaulting imagination. And worse than that he feared other moments when his memory for ordinary things would fail.

He let out a deep quivering sigh, and the girl looked at him curiously, then she turned away, and joined the others.

Wickham stared after them. It's all this trouble, it's got on my mind, he told himself. If that were all cleared up I might be able to concentrate again, but every time I open a book now I can hear that maniac shouting, and every time I think about work I hear those hideous catcalls. I can't seem to get it out of my mind, I know it's silly, but I can't help it.

Footsteps paused beside him and he looked up to encounter Hugo Coltman's gaze. He threw the flower-petals behind his back, but the other did not appear to notice. Wickham saw the haggard look bent upon him. Was something else wrong? Wickham scrambled to his feet.

'I've just received a telephone call from the hospital, Wickham. I thought you might like to know that your cousin is conscious. The operation has been performed and Bennett is progressing satisfactorily.'

Wickham's face lit up. 'Oh, thank you,

sir, that's good news.'

'Apparently he's quite cheerful. He sent a message that I was to tell you not to feel responsible for what happened.'

How much, Wickham wondered, did old Hugo know?

'Did Dicky say anything about — that is, did he have any idea who — who — ?'

'From what the nurse said, he had no idea at all who struck him,' Hugo Coltman said. 'He didn't see the person at all.' His mouth turned down at the corners. 'I must admit I'm disappointed. I'd hoped he might help the — er — investigation.'

'What are you going to do, sir?'

But the other might not have heard; his gaze had shifted to the blossom which had fallen from Wickham's fingers and lay scattered on the ground. He turned away and left the student staring after him.

Hugo Coltman went into the house and through to the outer office. Miss Frayle was not there, no doubt she was finishing a late breakfast after her experience last night. Coltman was

144

absently wondering when the workmen would put his study in order again, when his eye caught the morning's newspapers which lay on Miss Frayle's desk.

Still in a grey reverie he unfolded them, and then the staring headline of the local paper caught his eye. He gazed at the heavy type, then the fine, slender hand that held the sheets trembled. His face was very pale, a nerve throbbed in his forehead.

Mysterious Happenings at Local Drama Academy, he read. Wave of Terror Strikes Famous Actor's School.

He glanced up for a moment as Miss Frayle came in and stood there indecisively. She could see perspiration glistening on his brow. For a moment she wondered if he had been taken suddenly ill.

'Mr. Coltman,' she said. 'Are you all right? Shall I phone for Dr. Morelle?'

He waved the newspaper at her.

'Miss Frayle,' he said, and his voice was a harsh croak. 'How on earth has the *Gazette* got hold of this?'

She grabbed the paper and read what he indicated. 'How could they have heard?' she said incredulously.

The bleak unhappy eyes met hers, wide behind her spectacles. 'I don't know. I made it clear to everyone that they keep this matter to themselves.'

He began reading aloud, every word he uttered like a gasp of pain.

'A series of strange and unexplained incidents, culminating in a brutal attack on a student, has brought tension at Hugo Coltman's Drama Workshop to fever pitch. What seemed at first the work of a practical joker has taken on the appearance of an organized attack upon this famous dramatic academy, whose founder and head is Hugo Coltman, the noted actor.

'The first incident occurred three days ago, when a series of interruptions wrecked a lecture given by the celebrated psychiatrist and criminologist, Dr. Morelle. Two nights later, valuable paintings hung in the school theatre were slashed to pieces, and a sixteen-year-old student, Richard Bennett, who, presumably on the trail of the destroyer, had entered the theatre, was brutally attacked. He is now in hospital and there is every hope that he will recover.

'Meantime, Mr. Coltman is pursuing investigations that he hopes will lead to the capture of the guilty person. He assures me — '

Hugo Coltman broke off, incredulous. Miss Frayle gasped.

'But you haven't spoken to him, have you?'

'I have not, but I shall now.'

Grim-faced, Coltman ran his eye down the rest of the column, then threw the paper on one side with an exclamation and seized the telephone.

As he waited to be connected, first with the newspaper office, then with the editor, he stared unseeingly in front of him. Who could possibly have deliberately gone against his wishes and given this story to the newspaper? And why? The editor was at the other end of the line.

'Hugo Coltman here. I've just seen the *Gazette* and — '

There was a chuckle over the wire, interrupting him. 'I'm obliged to you for letting us in on it.'

Hugo Coltman could hardly believe his ears. He fumed incoherently for a moment, and then managed to choke out the words: 'Whoever gave you that story did so contrary to my expressed wish. I made it very apparent to my people here not to spread the story around. It would seem that everybody knows about our troubles now, thanks to your newspaper.'

'Just a minute.' The voice held a bewildered tone. 'It was you yourself who told me to run it. If you change your mind overnight, you can't blame me.'

'Are you mad?' It was Coltman's turn to sound baffled. 'I told you nothing. I've never spoken to you before.'

'Someone's played a trick on us,' the voice in his ear said. 'I had a telephone call late yesterday afternoon from somebody who said he was you. Hugo Coltman. He gave it me just as we ran it. You said — or whoever it was said — the business couldn't be hushed up any longer and they wanted to be sure we got the story right. But you say it wasn't you?'

'It certainly was not. Did it sound like me?'

'It was a man speaking. At the time I had no doubt it was you. Why should I? I'm extremely sorry, Mr. Coltman. I'd no idea the call wasn't genuine.'

Hugo Coltman stared helplessly in front of him, his cheeks gaunter than ever, it seemed to Miss Frayle. She stood watching, waves of pity for him overwhelming her. At last, with a sigh, and no further word he replaced the receiver.

This latest attack upon him was obviously aimed at his pride which now winced and shrank from the spotlight of publicity. Whoever had done this had known his character, and the accuracy and detail of the story pointed to the fact that it must have been someone at the Workshop who had spoken to the *Gazette* editor masquerading as himself.

Dejectedly, he slumped into a chair, and picked up the newspaper where Miss Frayle had let it fall on to the desk.

'Mysterious Happenings at Local Dramatic Academy. Wave of Terror Strikes Famous Actor's School.'

Miss Frayle felt she could read his thoughts. Here was punishment for his pride. She knew how bitter at heart he must feel as he stared at the lurid headline. Had he deserved to have his shame so publicly exposed? She sensed he was almost overwhelmed by a sense of his own helplessness.

'I'll get hold of Dr. Morelle,' she said.

16

Dr. Morelle got out of the Duesenberg and went up the short flight of steps. He had come straight from the hospital. There he had chatted to the nurse concerned who had passed on to him what Dicky Bennett had muttered during his first moments of consciousness after the operation, before falling into a sound sleep. That young Bennett had not been able to identify his assailant had not disappointed Dr. Morelle unduly; he would almost certainly have been attacked from behind and in darkness.

In the hall Dr. Morelle paused. A curiously searching throb of music came from the direction of the theatre. It was the sound of youthful voices.

Dr. Morelle made his way along the hall to the door which led into the theatre, and stood there for a few moments intrigued by the seemingly wordless chant. The deeper chords of the male voices beat out persistently under the wailing minor melody of the sopranos, and he wondered what inspiration had produced this strange theme.

No doubt the students were rehearsing something special for the end-of-term performance Miss Frayle had mentioned to him. Here was the deeper throb again, coming in now strong. They were singing in a triumphant major that jarred and swept the girls' chanting. Then the sopranos were dominant again, creeping by semitones up to a soaring height, wavering above the beating tones of the youths' voices. They hung there, dizzily, for bar after bar, then in a splintering sound, showered down to an easier pitch.

Dr. Morelle's expression was thoughtful as he turned back the way he had come. This must be the work that Roy Allen was engaged upon, he decided, from what he recalled Miss Frayle telling him. Certainly Allen had drawn a tremendous amount out of his young pupils. He remembered Miss Frayle saying something about how the music teacher was rehearsing the work, his own composition, in two halves, separately.

Dr. Morelle paused at a classroom door which was slightly open and heard the irritable tones of Theodore Willard putting his students through the hoop.

'How many times must I tell you, Bellamy,' Willard was saying, 'not to mumble as if you had a mouthful of hot potato? Take that line again.' Dr. Morelle listened to the student repeating the phrase, stumbling and stuttering.

'How can I be expected to teach diction to such an incompetent lout?' he heard Willard shout. The irascible voice continued in a quieter tone: 'Anderson, perhaps you can do better with it?'

The student named Anderson reeled off the required phrase in a style which was more to Willard's satisfaction, and Dr. Morelle moved on.

He reached another classroom as a group of students poured out for a break. Young girls and young men, fresh and lively, in a variety of practice clothes. Some of the girls glanced at the gaunt, silent figure boldly and impudently, while others were chattering and laughing.

'Why Finch should get in such a state,' Dr. Morelle heard one girl say, 'just because you can't get her idea right first time, I don't know. She really was stark raving at times.'

'Perhaps she's been crossed in love,' some other girl said.

The students hurried off. There was no doubt that the atmosphere of Hugo Coltman's academy was dramatic enough, Dr. Morelle thought sardonically. At any rate, the teachers seemed to be on edge. Then Elspeth Finch appeared, a graceful figure in the practice blouse and tights, but a frown marring her olive features. She saw him and stopped.

'A word with you,' he said smoothly.

'It'll have to be a word,' she said. 'I haven't much time.'

He thought he detected an uneasiness in her expression. Her eyes flickered from his face over his shoulder, as if she wished someone to appear and interrupt them.

'I merely wanted to inquire,' he said mildly, 'why so interested in the 'School For Scandal' photograph in Hugo Coltman's study?'

Elspeth Finch gasped as if he had struck her. Her eyes narrowed to blazing slits.

'What the devil's it got to do with you?' she said. 'I mentioned to your nosy Miss Frayle that I was interested in all the photos. I just happened to be looking at them. I've noticed them before when I've been in old Hugo's office.'

'Was your interest so strong that you thought you'd like to borrow one?'

'Borrow one?' Her voice rose. 'What are you getting at? I never touched any of the damned things.'

'Then I was mistaken,' Dr. Morelle said.

He watched her go and smiled a little thinly to himself. Crossed in love? he wondered, recalling the joking remark made just now by one of the students.

Who would Elspeth Finch give her love to, he mused; more important, who would reciprocate the sort of affection of which she was capable? Dr. Morelle needed little understanding of the riddle of the human heart to be certain that Elspeth Finch's passion would run deep and take some eluding. The man she settled for would have to fight like a trapped animal to escape her.

A few minutes later he was in Miss Frayle's office, listening to Hugo Coltman's account of what he had read in the local newspaper and his phone conversation with the editor. Miss Frayle, after remaining for a few minutes after Dr. Morelle's arrival, had gone about her duties elsewhere.

'It is certain,' Coltman was saying, 'that it must have been one of my staff who spoke to the editor.'

Dr. Morelle nodded. 'Obviously someone,' he said, who could impersonate you successfully enough over the phone; while the accuracy and detail of the story printed proves it was a person familiar with every happening.'

'But which of them is it?' Coltman said.

'I had already decided that the circle of suspects must be narrowed down to a small group of people, your teachers,' Dr. Morelle said. 'Although there still remains the possibility that an especially talented and resourceful student may be the guilty party.'

'Whatever it costs, we must find the devil.' Hugo Coltman banged his fist on the desk. 'This,' he crumpled the newspaper up and threw it to the floor, 'this is the final straw.'

A few minutes later, leaving Coltman to carry on with his routine work, Dr. Morelle went out into the hall and made his way thoughtfully towards the large glazed doors flung open to the garden. He could still hear the sounds of music and chanting voices from the direction of the theatre. Once the music and voices stopped and he thought he could hear Roy Allen's voice raised in criticism.

Dr. Morelle went out into the garden. He lit a Le Sphinx. A voice behind him caused him to turn. It was Isobel Ross holding a cigarette, and smiling at him.

'Could you give me a light, Dr. Morelle?'

He flicked his lighter and held the flame to her cigarette. She nodded her thanks, and took a grateful drag. He noticed that the fingers holding the cigarette trembled a little.

'That was good,' she said. Then, after a

pause, she spoke again suddenly, as if she had just made up her mind about something.

'I wonder if you can help me? It's one of my students,' she went on. 'He's a nervy type, there's nothing in that for a would-be actor, but he seems to have lost control over his memory. He's got very brilliant prospects — or he had — now his memory lets him down. Yesterday he seemed to have a complete blackout during a speech, which ordinarily he would manage with no difficulty at all.'

'If he's an emotional type as you suggest,' Dr. Morelle said, 'it may be merely a matter of strain. No doubt he fears the end-of-term results which will affect his future.'

'You think it may be nothing more than that?'

'Without examining the young man,' Dr. Morelle said, 'I can't, of course, offer any opinion. But I imagine it is a fairly typical case of natural anxiety at this particular time. If you are really worried, however, I should advise him to take medical advice.'

Isobel Ross nodded again. 'I am sure that what you say is right, Doctor.' A faint pause, then: 'I did at one time wonder if he'd had anything to do with the trouble here.'

Dr. Morelle said nothing. A cloud of smoke from his Le Sphinx rose and disintegrated in the sunlight.

'It — it's such a strange business,' she said, 'and it's upset him; you see, he's Dicky Bennett's cousin. And the attack on Dicky seems to prey on his mind, he feels responsible for what happened.'

Dr. Morelle's eyes were fixed on her. For a moment she was reminded of some hooded-eyed eagle waiting to swoop, then as if mesmerized by his unwinking stare she found herself telling him the whole story, as she knew it, of Brian Wickham. When she had finished he nodded sympathetically.

'What you say,' he said, 'confirms the impression you gave me at first. That as a result of his vivid imagination and great sensibility, and his anxiety about his future in the theatre, Wickham might be particularly susceptible to nervous or mental strain. It seems likely, too, that recent events have contributed to his nervous upset. You should keep an eye on him, and if you still feel concerned on his behalf, insist that he sees his doctor. I feel sure there is nothing seriously amiss, and that when the trouble here is cleared up, and he begins his holiday, all will be well with him.'

'Thanks, Dr. Morelle,' Isobel Ross said. 'I will do what you say.'

'As for the possibility that Wickham is concerned with the mystery that has descended upon the Drama Workshop,' Dr. Morelle said, 'I think you may dismiss that notion from your mind.'

Isobel Ross gave him a little smile and taking another drag at her cigarette moved away.

Dr. Morelle watched her return to the house, his expression speculative. Then slowly he retraced his footsteps.

Meanwhile, Miss Frayle, her thoughts preoccupied with the events that had descended upon the Drama Workshop, was returning from the theatre, where she had gone to check up on some details

connected with the end-of-term programme, to her office.

Anxious to enjoy the bright morning
sunshine, she had taken the longer way
through the garden, instead of going
through from the theatre. As she moved
noiselessly across the lawn towards the
gravel path leading to the house, she was
brought to a halt by voices coming to her
from behind a tall hedge which hid the
speakers from her view. She could make
out the voice of Elspeth Finch, cool and
mocking, with its inevitable edge, but the
answering voice was a low mumble.

'My dear man,' Elspeth was saying, 'don't
make such a tragedy of it. Everything
must come to an end.'

Miss Frayle lost the end of the words,
it was as if Elspeth Finch had turned
away. She caught the man's tones again,
but they were too indistinct to catch.
Instinctively Miss Frayle moved on,
she had no intention of eavesdropping
upon what was obviously a private
conversation. Then Elspeth Finch's laugh
came to her.

'Throwing you over?' Miss Frayle

caught the sharp tones again. 'Don't use such crude phrases, my dear. We can still be friends. It isn't the end of the world.'

Again the man's voice now it seemed with an undertone of angry resentment in it.

Despite her uneasiness at eavesdropping, Miss Frayle paused to try and distinguish the owner of the voice, then she thought she heard the sound of footsteps on the other side of the hedge approaching and she hurried away, overwhelmed at the thought of being caught eavesdropping.

Quickly she turned the corner of the house, her shoes crunching on the gravel path, and without looking round she went into the hall. Elspeth Finch, she thought, but who was the man? She shrugged to herself, it was really no concern of hers.

But when she found Dr. Morelle leaving Hugo Coltman to return to the town, she walked with him to the car and she did not forget to tell him of this snatch of conversation she had overheard in the garden. Dr. Morelle had been eyeing Hugo Coltman's dejected figure vanish into the shadows of the hall. It seemed he had barely been paying any attention to what Miss Frayle had been saying. But now he swung on her, his eyes narrowed, his face alert.

'Are you sure you can't name the man?'

She shook her head. She wished now she had worried less about being caught eavesdropping and had made a determined effort to learn the identity of the owner of that second voice.

'There are evidences of strong passions running beneath the surface here,' Dr. Morelle said. 'And you did not think it necessary to discover who this man might be — '

'But, Doctor,' Miss Frayle interrupted him, hurt by his implied criticism. 'It couldn't be one of the teachers here.'

He frowned at her. 'What makes you think that?' he said.

'Because,' she said triumphantly, 'she's quarrelled and snapped at every man in the place, except Roy Allen. But he wouldn't have anything to do with her.'

'Whatever confidence may be placed in your conclusion,' he said, 'I happen to have heard Allen with his class only a little earlier on, anyway. But it could have been any of the other teachers — since you cannot be sure whose voice it was, you cannot be sure whose voice it wasn't.'

Again Miss Frayle wished fervently she had overcome her scruples and discovered the identity of the man with Elspeth Finch. Although she reasoned, she couldn't quite see what it could have to do with the recent happenings at the Drama Workshop.

'Miss Ross has been discussing one of her students with me,' Dr. Morelle said. 'A harassed, somewhat highly-strung young man named Brian Wickham.'

'What on earth — ?' Miss Frayle said, and then broke off. 'Surely she doesn't think Brian Wickham — ?'

'Apparently he has been behaving somewhat strangely,' Dr. Morelle said. 'I was able to reassure her that there didn't appear to be anything to worry about.'

'He is a nervy type,' Miss Frayle said. 'But after all, he's an actor, or wants to be one. A nervous temperament must be part of his stock-in-trade.'

'From what's been going on here,' Dr. Morelle said, 'I find myself irresistibly bound to agree with every word you say.'

Miss Frayle blushed with pleasure. 'He's her star pupil,' she said, 'so I expect she feels anxious about him. This should be his last term here, and if he does well at the end-of-term show, he could land himself with a good contract.'

'In that case,' Dr. Morelle said reflectively, 'it's a little odd, don't you think, that Miss Ross should have even hinted that he might be implicated in the unpleasantness here?'

Miss Frayle thought she detected a tone in his voice with which in the past she had been not unfamiliar. She stared at him, her eyes wide behind her horn-rims.

'You don't mean,' she said, 'that she was trying to turn your suspicions on to him?'

'If that were the case,' he said drily, 'it would imply that Isobel Ross was seeking to direct suspicion from herself, and why, Miss Frayle, should she do that?'

'Only if she was mixed up in all these goings-on,' Miss Frayle said.

'Or that she was shielding someone else,' Dr. Morelle said, 'whom she knew, or thought she knew was involved.'

Miss Frayle clutched impulsively at his arm. 'Do you suspect her?' she said. 'Or someone else that she's covering up?'

Dr. Morelle surveyed her calmly. 'So far,' he said, 'the only person I don't suspect in this whole affair is you: otherwise anyone, even Hugo Coltman himself, could be guilty.'

17

Dr. Morelle had a lunch appointment in London and at midday he drove away in the rakish-looking, yellow Duesenberg. He would be back early afternoon.

The blue skies clouded over after lunch so that when Miss Frayle, with some shopping to do in the town, set off, she wondered whether to take her raincoat or not. She decided against it, estimating that the storm in the air wouldn't develop for two or three hours, when she intended to be back at the Workshop in readiness for Dr. Morelle's return.

As she turned out of the entrance-gate she saw Isobel Ross ahead of her. At first she thought to call out with the object of accompanying her into the town, since she too was going in that direction. Then she changed her mind and remained silent, keeping Isobel Ross in view, walking behind her.

The woman ahead was walking quickly.

It was about half a mile to the town, and presently Isobel Ross was lost to Miss Frayle's view. Without quite knowing why, Miss Frayle quickened her pace. She found the air suddenly hot and stifling. She felt the palms of her hands become moist and she dabbed her upper lip with her handkerchief. Was the early summer heatwave about to break in a storm? It would be a relief, she thought.

She rounded the corner and then stopped. Some fifty or sixty yards ahead Isobel Ross stood, and beyond her, her back to Isobel and Miss Frayle, there was Elspeth Finch, sitting on a low gate. She was obviously waiting for someone. The man she had been talking to that morning? Miss Frayle experienced a tremor of excitement. She drew into the side of the footpath which ran along the lonely road.

Isobel Ross, too, moved closer to the hedge overhung with the branches of trees, as if she was seeking concealment. There was an air of suppressed impatience about Elspeth Finch which was not lost on the two secretly watching her.

Anybody would think she was waiting for a boy-friend, Miss Frayle thought. Which didn't add up to what she'd over-heard that morning. Then she started, as Roy Allen appeared at the gate. He had obviously been walking across the fields, poring over the manuscript which was under his arm. He looked startled as Elspeth jumped off the gate, and seemed to pull himself away from her grasp. But she was persistent, she pulled open the gate and accompanied Roy Allen back the way he had come. They went out of sight.

She seems determined to get her hooks into him, Miss Frayle mused. Waylaying him like that. Then she saw Isobel Ross draw closer still to the hedge. A man had come out of the gate on the other side of the road, opposite the gate through which Elspeth and the unwilling Roy had gone.

It was Theodore Willard. He paused, looking across the road at the retreating pair. Then he crossed the road, opened the gate and halted irresolutely.

Miss Frayle could see Willard's narrow face, so busy was he watching Roy Allen and Elspeth Finch that he did not notice he was himself being watched. Suddenly he closed the gate and went off at a rapid pace along the road towards the town.

He's decided not to spy on the two love-birds, Miss Frayle thought, and she moved away from the hedge forgetting for the moment that Isobel Ross was ahead of her. Her sudden movement must have caught the other woman's eye, for she whipped round. She saw Miss Frayle and waved to her.

Feeling a little foolish, Miss Frayle moved towards her.

'Did you see what I saw?' Isobel Ross called out to her as she approached, and Miss Frayle heard a friendly note in her voice.

Miss Frayle smiled uncertainly. 'I'm afraid I just stood and stared for all I was worth,' she said.

'Me, too,' Isobel Ross said frankly. 'It seems Roy's going to find it hard to escape from Elspeth.'

Miss Frayle was looking anxiously at the sky. Ahead of them was an ominous mass of black, and the air seemed very still. She and Isobel were walking along together, and now they reached the gate to the field. Elspeth Finch and Roy Allen were nowhere to be seen.

The field ran away to a wooded hillside and was bounded by a great hedge which zigzagged untidily, so that anyone keeping close to it could be hidden from the road for long stretches.

Isobel Ross glanced up at the sky. 'I don't know about you,' she said, 'but I'm turning back. One hell of a storm's brewing and I don't intend to get caught in it. My shopping can wait till to-morrow.' Miss Frayle agreed and together they turned back the way they had come.

The first great drops of rain splashed down as they hurried up the drive to the Drama Workshop. Breathless, they dashed inside the hall as a crash of thunder split the sky. Lightning flashed into the sudden gloom.

'I wonder how Elspeth's getting on?' Miss Frayle said.

Isobel Ross laughed. 'I should think even her burning passion for her beloved Roy will get damped in this lot.'

The storm rolled and crashed around the house. Rain slanted across the drive, and Miss Frayle, peering out through the streaming window of her office, saw the trees lashed by sudden driving squalls.

Within an hour the storm had passed. Miss Frayle pushed open the window and breathed in the freshened, rain-cooled air. Reminder of the tumult that had gone was a throbbing in her head, and a garden dismal with flattened plants, scattered flower blooms and pools of water. But birds were singing again and the sky, a washed-out pale blue, was soft and beautiful to look at, and her eyes rose to it gratefully.

It'll be wet underfoot, she thought, the idea of going out for a few moments occurring to her, but I don't think it'll rain again.

She heard the swish of a raincoat and she saw Isobel Ross swinging into view. The other caught sight of her and crossed to the window.

'Leave your blessed office,' she said, 'and come for that walk you didn't have earlier.'

'I'm waiting for Dr. Morelle to get back from London,' Miss Frayle said. 'Anyway it'll be soaking underfoot.'

'I'll be all right,' Isobel Ross said. 'See you at tea.'

Miss Frayle watched her go, and then turned to her desk.

Five minutes later Isobel Ross was swinging along a narrow road that wound between dripping hedges. A faint breeze carried the sound of a church clock to her. Three-fifteen. Was that all? It seemed hours since the storm had broken.

Her spirits rose as she walked, the storm seemed to have cleared the doubts and worries that had beset her during the past few days. She came to a stretch of meadow which rose to the bulk of a great hill, covered with trees whose many-shaded green frothed to the skyline. These were Greenacre Woods.

Isobel Ross swished through long grass and took a winding path up the hill.

Suddenly a figure came running and stumbling down the path, having burst from some undergrowth to the right, and for a moment Isobel's heart leaped. Then she said: 'Wickham, what on earth are you doing here?'

Brian Wickham stopped in his tracks, staring at her stupidly. His clothes were soaked and splashed with mud. His bedraggled hair hung over his forehead. He looked as if he had been out in the rain for hours. She was startled by his dazed expression as he looked at her.

'What's the matter?' she said sharply.

He passed a hand across his forehead vaguely. 'I'm all right,' he said. 'I just didn't seem quite sure where I am, that's all. I came out just before lunch, for a walk.'

'You must be wet to the skin.'

Wickham smiled vaguely. 'It's all right, really. I enjoyed it. It was terrific, the storm.'

'If you've been out here since before lunch, you must have walked miles.'

'I suppose I have,' he said. 'Don't ask me where I've been, I just don't know. I was walking . . . thinking . . . trying to remember . . . '

'You'd better get back home,' she said, 'and get out of those wet things.'

She broke off, frowning at him. He was standing there, his eyes fixed in a faraway, intent gaze.

'All I can remember,' he said, 'are trees. Dripping trees, and cold drops falling on my face, and my feet tangled in the long grass. Once I must have fallen because I found myself on my face where two paths join, tripped, I suppose.'

'I'd better come back with you,' Isobel said.

She was walking alongside him. He looked at her, his expression still half-dazed. 'I must have had a blackout, the same as I did in class.'

At the back of Isobel Ross's mind was the thought that Dr. Morelle would have returned from London by now. She would like him to have talked to Wickham before he went home.

They got back to the Drama Workshop and she saw the Duesenberg draw up by the front porch. While Wickham sat shivering a little in the dining-room, a hot cup of tea in his hands, Isobel went in search of Dr. Morelle. She thought he might be in Miss Frayle's office.

She reached the door which was a little open and heard Miss Frayle talking to Dr. Morelle; she could hear the fussiness in her tone as she persuaded him to have another cup of tea. Anyone would think, Isobel Ross smiled to herself, that Dr. Morelle had arrived from far-off Tibet, through hazardous storms and desert droughts, instead of from thirty-miles' distant London, with a bit of a rainstorm on the way.

She decided not to disturb Miss Frayle's obvious enjoyment of her rôle of ministering angel, and turned away from the office and went back to Brian Wickham in the dining-room. 'A good night's rest,' she said to him. 'And unless you really feel up to it, I don't expect to see you in class to-morrow.'

18

'Hallo, Isobel.' It was Jeff Sullivan who greeted Isobel Ross as she came into the common-room next morning. She gave him a smile and glanced at Roy Allen and Theodore Willard who were looking at her with mild interest.

'What's this I hear about your star pupil?' Willard said.

'Wickham?' Isobel said. 'It's nothing serious. I found him wandering round in the woods, after the storm. He seems better this morning, though his memory is a bit of a blank.'

'A blank?' Roy Allen said. 'What d'you mean?'

'He insists on coming in to school, though I must say work seems to be of little value to him at the moment.' She glanced at Sullivan. 'Seen Elspeth?'

'Come to think of it,' he said lightly, 'I haven't.'

'She's very late,' Isobel said.

'Can't say I was looking very hard for her,' Roy Allen said, scowling. 'Blessed woman. I've got enough on my mind as it is.'

'She'll be here soon enough,' Willard said, his voice rasping, and turning away from the others. 'Snapping around like a spoilt lap-dog, so let's be thankful while she's still absent. I bet her class is happy about it.'

'I found her lot wandering around,' Isobel said. 'I sent one of the girls to report to Hugo. Elspeth may be ill.'

'I hope not,' Roy Allen said. 'Hasn't she got an invalid mother to look after, or something?'

'Yes,' Isobel said.

Hugo Coltman was at that moment bent over some papers on his desk in his study. The room was tidied and only awaited the house-decorators who would be arriving next week to restore it to its former state of comfort. Coltman looked up from his desk.

'Yes, Miss Frayle?'

'It's about Miss Finch. One of the girls from her class has reported that she

178

hasn't arrived this morning. I was just wondering what we ought to do.'

Hugo Coltman frowned. 'She must have been called away last night and not had time to get in touch with us.'

'Her mother was going into a nursing-home to-day or tomorrow,' Miss Frayle said.

'Perhaps you'd be kind enough to call at Miss Finch's home, Miss Frayle? Send for a taxi and go right away.'

About thirty minutes later Miss Frayle found the house, one of a row in a leafy lane on the other side of the town. She asked the taxi to wait, while she went up the brick path and knocked at the door. The door was opened by a brisk, competent woman whom Miss Frayle recognized at once as a district nurse.

'Yes?'

'I'm from the Drama Workshop,' said Miss Frayle. 'Miss Finch, one of our teachers, hasn't turned up.'

The nurse looked at her oddly. 'You'd better come in,' she said quietly.

With a sudden feeling of foreboding, Miss Frayle went into the hall.

'Has anything happened?' she said.

'Bad news, I'm afraid,' the nurse said. 'A next-door neighbour heard Mrs. Finch, Miss Finch's mother, calling out this morning. The neighbour kept an eye on Mrs. Finch, who, as you may know, is an invalid, so she hurried in. She found Mrs. Finch in a distressed state. Her daughter hadn't come home.'

'Good gracious,' Miss Frayle's hand went to her agitated glasses. 'What happened to her?'

'The neighbour called the police, and that's why I'm here.' The nurse paused, then she went on. 'This will be a shock for you, I'm afraid. The police had already learned that a woman had been found early this morning in Greenacre Woods. The body was identified as Miss Finch.'

Miss Frayle's mind was reeling. She could only mutter something dazedly.

'The old lady doesn't know the full facts of the case yet,' the nurse said. 'She was due to go into a nursing-home today; in any case, it will be quite impossible for her to live here alone, without help.'

The thought clouded Miss Frayle's

mind: Could this be yet one more terrible jest, one more blow at the Hugo Coltman Drama Workshop? Rapidly pushing this thought from her mind, she said: 'I'll tell Mr. Coltman, he'll be terribly upset, of course. If there's anything we can do to help Mrs. Finch — ' Miss Frayle floundered, her brain a maelstrom of questions.

'Thank you,' the nurse said.

Miss Frayle rushed to the taxi and headed back for the Workshop.

She hoped to see Dr. Morelle's car in the drive as the taxi turned into the gates. Her heart leapt at the sight of the familiar, low-built yellow car; then her spirits drooped again as she saw alongside it a black saloon car waiting by the porch steps, and as she got out of her taxi and paid it off she saw the uniformed police-driver at the wheel of the black saloon.

She dashed into the hall in time to see one of the maidservants ushering two men into her office.

'Two gentlemen who wanted to see you, sir,' she heard the girl say.

Miss Frayle shot in after the two men,

past the maid-servant and saw Dr. Morelle silhouetted against the study window. He raised an eyebrow as he glanced at her. Hugo Coltman on the other side of his desk had just stood up, his face darkened by a heavy frown.

'I suppose you've called about that story in the *Gazette*?' he said. 'I must say that I consider it is not a police matter at all.'

'It isn't that,' Miss Frayle heard herself say, and checked herself.

Dr. Morelle gave her a sharp look. Then he turned to the two men as the elder one said to Coltman: 'I'm Detective-Inspector Pockett, sir. This is Detective-Sergeant Hopkins. We are police officers. I'm afraid there is more involved,' he went on, 'than the matters mentioned in the local newspaper.'

At the detective's words all arrogance left Hugo Coltman and there was a hunted look in his eyes. Dr. Morelle's expression was urbane as he bent it upon the two plain-clothes men, both of whom regarded him with fresh interest as Coltman introduced him to them. And Miss Frayle blushed a little and fiddled with her glasses as they smiled at her.

Pockett was middle-aged, a stocky, solid figure in his brown suit. His large round head was going bald with wisps of greying hair across it. His sunburnt face had a tight mouth under a heavy iron-grey moustache. The sergeant was taller, lean and dark, and clean-shaven, with alert grey eyes. Both had an air of quiet competence and watchfulness.

'What else could it be, other than what you've read in the newspaper,' Hugo Coltman said, 'unless — ?' He broke off, then went on: 'I don't understand you, Inspector.'

'Don't you see, Mr. Coltman,' Miss Frayle said agitatedly, 'it's to do with — '

'You'd better remain silent, Miss Frayle,' Dr. Morelle said. 'I imagine our visitors will tell us all we want to know.'

'I understand, sir,' Inspector Pockett said, with a glance at Dr. Morelle, 'that a Miss Elspeth Finch was on your staff?'

Hugo Coltman started. 'Did you say Miss Finch *was* on my staff? She *is* on my staff.'

He turned to look inquiringly at Miss Frayle. His head came back with a jerk as Inspector Pockett spoke slowly, his face expressionless.

'Her body was found in Greenacre Woods this morning.'

Coltman's face went a deathly pallor.

Miss Frayle's gaze turned to Dr. Morelle, whose expression did not change by a flicker. It was almost as if he had been forewarned of what had happened.

She turned her horn-rims back upon Inspector Pockett as he continued. 'A workman found her this morning. She had been dead some hours.' He paused for a moment, then he said: 'My own investigations indicate that the time of her death was in the early afternoon.'

Hugo Coltman could only continue to stare at him, his mouth quivering.

'May we know how this unfortunate woman died?' It was Dr. Morelle who asked the question, the answer to which Miss Frayle dreaded to hear. Though she knew what it must be.

The Inspector glanced at Dr. Morelle, then at the detective-sergeant. It was obvious that he was weighing up how much he should divulge at this stage. Evidently Dr. Morelle's presence assured him.

'She had been strangled,' he said, 'manually.'

'My God,' Coltman groaned, and half collapsed into a chair. 'Murder?'

'I'm afraid so, sir,' Inspector Pockett said. 'I've been placed in charge of the case, with Detective-Sergeant Hopkins here. We shall, of course, conduct our inquiries with the least possible trouble to you.'

'I can't believe it,' Coltman said thickly. 'Who on earth can have wished to harm her?'

Miss Frayle echoed his words. Who could have wanted to murder poor Elspeth Finch? Acid-tongued, sharp-voiced she may have been, but it seemed incredible that she could have incurred such deadly hatred on the part of anyone that they could have done her to death.

In her mind's eye she saw Elspeth Finch at the gate by the field with Roy Allen, little could she have foreseen then that it was to be the last time that she would see her alive. She wondered if Isobel Ross would be terribly upset when she heard the news.

'That is what we have to find out,' Inspector Pockett was saying. 'I hope I can rely on any assistance you may be able to give us.'

'Of course,' Hugo Coltman said. Then he glanced up. 'You surely don't imagine that it could be anyone at my Workshop? It seems obvious that it was the work of some stranger poor Miss Finch encountered.'

Inspector Pockett pursed his lips non-committally. 'We shall have to question her associates here,' he said. 'It will be important to learn as much as possible about her background, her work and her private life.'

'I'm sure you will find Mr. Coltman and all the members of his staff only too anxious to help you,' Dr. Morelle said with a side-long glance at the figure hunched in his chair. Coltman raised his head and gave an affirmative nod, and then sank his face in his hands.

'It is possible,' Inspector Pockett said, 'that it was a chance meeting with someone, a thief or some unbalanced person which resulted in murder, but,' he shrugged his heavy shoulders, 'the indications are that it wasn't that type of assault.'

'How shall we be able to carry on now?' Hugo Coltman said, half to himself.

'As best you can,' Dr. Morelle said.

'Everyone will do all they can to help,' Miss Frayle said, touched by the sight of that crumpled figure, and Coltman gave her a wan smile of gratitude.

Inspector Pockett was watching Hugo Coltman, who had raised his head and whose gaze was fixed unseeingly out of the window.

It seemed to Miss Frayle that he was trying to will Elspeth Finch to cross the lawn and approach the study, so that the latest horror adding up to the nightmare which enveloped the Drama Workshop would be dissipated.

'Incidentally,' the detective said, 'that story in the *Gazette*, it seems this business about poor Miss Finch isn't the first lot of trouble to hit you. Have you found out who was responsible for what's been happening here?'

'Surely,' Coltman said, 'that can have no connection with this ghastly tragedy? If that's what you're hinting at?'

'I wasn't hinting at anything, sir,' Inspector Pockett said pleasantly. 'But does it occur to you that they may be linked in some way?'

Hugo Coltman stood up and looked at Dr. Morelle, then at Miss Frayle. His staring eyes came to rest finally upon the two police officers.

'It can't be,' he said to Pockett. He passed his hand across his forehead, then he turned to Dr. Morelle again. 'Dr. Morelle here, of whom you have heard, had very kindly come down from London at my request to begin to investigate the atrocious happenings referred to in the newspaper report.'

'I'm very glad you're here, Doctor,' Inspector Pockett said warmly. 'It's a lucky break for us that you have been on the spot.'

Dr. Morelle favoured the detective with

a deprecatory smile. Then he glanced at Hugo Coltman. 'You will appreciate that Mr. Coltman is very shaken by this tragic business coming on top of the other unpleasantness. I suggest that between us, Miss Frayle and I can tell you all that might be of any assistance to you so far as the Drama Workshop is concerned.'

Inspector Pockett nodded in agreement. 'That will certainly make a good start.' He glanced at the detective-sergeant then turned to Hugo Coltman. 'Since Dr. Morelle can give us an outline of the general situation here — '

'I leave it entirely in his hands,' Coltman said shakily. 'Forgive me, Inspector, if I appear to be tending to think mostly of the effect of these dreadful happenings on my Workshop. Though, of course, this unfortunate end of poor Elspeth Finch — ' He broke off, then he said: 'If I may leave you with Dr. Morelle and Miss Frayle?'

'Certainly, sir. The body is in the mortuary,' Inspector Pockett said. 'If you would consent to make a formal identification for us? I'll have my driver take you along in the car.'

'Of course. Her mother hasn't been told, I presume?'

'No, she's in a nursing-home. I understand she's seriously ill.' The detective turned to the sergeant. 'Just see Mr. Coltman to the car.'

Squaring his shoulders, Hugo Coltman walked with dignity from the study, followed by Hopkins.

'That's better,' Inspector Pockett said, with a frank smile at Dr. Morelle, and then at Miss Frayle. 'I'm sure you will understand, Dr. Morelle, that we like to think we're every bit as good as the London fellows. I hope to solve this without the Chief Constable having to call in Scotland Yard, it'll be a feather in our caps, and with your help I think we might get away with it.'

'I am entirely at your disposal,' Dr. Morelle said suavely.

Detective-Sergeant Hopkins came in and closed the door quietly behind him.

The Inspector's features became graver, and Miss Frayle experienced a sudden shiver of excitement; once more, it

190

seemed, she was on to a murder investigation with Dr. Morelle.

Dr. Morelle lit a Le Sphinx thoughtfully. Through a cloud of smoke he said: 'I did not anticipate that the investigation I had undertaken here was to end in murder.' He contemplated the tip of his cigarette for a moment. 'It still does not seem in character with the other incidents which have been perpetrated.'

'There was this youngster, Bennett,' Sergeant Hopkins said. 'According to the newspaper, he got knocked about.'

Dr. Morelle nodded. 'I had felt,' he said, 'that the attack upon him was unpremeditated.' He paused, and then continued: 'Perhaps you would give me fuller details of the Miss Finch tragedy?'

19

'This workman,' Inspector Pockett said, 'was going through the woods at about seven a.m. on his way to the building estate the other side of the woods. He was noting the damage yesterday's storm had done to one or two trees, and he literally stumbled across the body. Lying face downwards it was, the head and shoulders half covered by some bushes, as if it had been pushed under them.'

Miss Frayle could not repress a shudder as the word-picture describing the discovery of the dead woman filled her mind. She recalled her last impression of her, alive and vital, her figure triumphant as she led Roy Allen through the gate into the field.

'The man started to drag her clear,' the detective continued. 'He thought at first she was ill, or just some drunk, who was sleeping it off. Then he saw the state of her face, the bruisemarks on her neck.'

'You were able to learn nothing from them?' Dr. Morelle said.

Inspector Pockett shook his head regretfully. 'Nothing except that the murderer wore gloves. Anyway it gave the man a bit of a shock, she wasn't a pleasant sight, as you can imagine.' He glanced across at Miss Frayle, and hesitated. 'He ran and found the nearest phone box and called us at once. I was sent for, and Hopkins and I went out immediately with the police surgeon, photographer, all the bag of tricks. He came to the conclusion she had been killed quite early the previous afternoon. She was completely soaked, Doctor, and you will remember the storm?'

Dr. Morelle nodded in agreement. 'That would help to fix the time of the murder,' he said.

Again the Inspector threw a look at Miss Frayle. 'The woman's clothes had not been disturbed in any way, so we can rule out that kind of assault.'

'Robbery?' Dr. Morelle said.

The other shook his head. 'Her hand-bag was lying open near her, indicating a struggle. There were one or two letters in the bag, a powder-compact, lipstick, a few coins and a couple of pound notes. She was wearing a white blouse and green skirt, and there was one of those light plastic raincoats near her. Fine nylon stockings, high-heeled shoes,' he stopped. He rubbed his moustache with a thick forefinger. 'Come to think of it,' he said, 'not very suitable clothes for a walk in the woods on a wet afternoon.'

Miss Frayle made a move forward as if to say something, and the detective-sergeant glanced at her questioningly.

'That was what Miss Finch was wearing when I saw her go through the gate with Roy Allen,' Miss Finch said.

'You saw her, Miss Frayle?' The Inspector looked at her sharply, then he eyed Dr. Morelle. 'This is important,' he said. 'You may have been one of the last people to see her alive.'

'We both saw her, Isobel Ross and I,' Miss Frayle said.

'If I may interrupt,' Dr. Morelle said. 'Inspector, Miss Frayle will give you a detailed account of what she and

Miss Ross, one of the teachers here, saw yesterday afternoon. But first I would be glad if you would continue with your own observations. I would like to get the picture of this scene perfectly clear in my mind. You were able to learn nothing from the vicinity surrounding the body?'

'The ground had been churned up. Miss Finch had struggled with her killer, and one of her shoes was kicked off.'

Again Miss Frayle shuddered, thinking of Elspeth Finch's last desperate battle for life, the breath being choked from her as her dark eyes, now bulging in her distorted face, took their last look into the eyes of her murderer. All memories of the wretched woman's unpleasant character were wiped away by the horror of her end.

'The man who found her added to the churning up of the ground,' Pockett said. 'He was wearing hob-nailed boots, when he began moving the body he trampled over a lot of impressions that might otherwise have been left.'

'Her handbag gave you nothing?' Dr.

Morelle said. 'Only her name and address on the letters?'

'There was a folded photograph in her handbag, some theatrical group. This man Hugo Coltman was in it,' Pockett said slowly.

Inspector Pockett's head came up with a jerk and the detective-sergeant looked up sharply as Dr. Morelle moved forward like some tall bird of prey about to pounce.

'A photograph?' Dr. Morelle said. 'Would it be a group of actors and actresses dressed in the clothes of a 'School For Scandal' production?'

'They were fancy-dress clothes,' the detective-sergeant said. Inspector Pockett turned to him and indicated the briefcase, which the other had placed on a chair. Nodding, Hopkins snapped it open and handed Dr. Morelle the photograph.

'Tested for fingerprints,' he said. 'Only those of the deceased on it.'

Miss Frayle, tingling with excitement, watched Dr. Morelle take the photograph and peer at it with narrowed eyes.

'So she did lie to me,' he said softly,

'when she said she hadn't taken it.'

Inspector Pockett and the detective-sergeant looked at him with puzzled interest.

'You think this may have something to do with the case?' Pockett said.

'If it has any significance,' Dr. Morelle said, 'that Miss Finch was silenced because of some knowledge she had gained from it, the murderer would have removed it, since the murderer had obviously searched her handbag.' He paused reflectively. 'In fact,' he went on, 'it is possible that this photograph had no part in the woman's death at all. She may have removed it through some fancy, perhaps she had a secret admiration for Hugo Coltman in this particular rôle? Who knows? Who can tell what goes on in a woman's mind?'

And Dr. Morelle turned a blandly contemplative gaze upon Miss Frayle.

20

Some thirty minutes later, Detective-Sergeant Hopkins closed the notebook full of shorthand notes that he had held on his knee. 'Fine lot of goings-on there's been at this place,' he said and glanced across at the Inspector. Hopkins had been engaged in taking down everything that Dr. Morelle, aided admirably by Miss Frayle, had been telling Pockett of the happenings at the Hugo Coltman Drama Workshop, as they knew it.

'He should have called in the police at the start of it all,' Hopkins said. 'Who knows it might have saved the Finch woman's life?'

'I saw Coltman's point of view,' Dr. Morelle said. 'He wanted to avoid unpleasant publicity for his dramatic academy at a time, the breaking-up of term, when it was particularly important that there should be no suggestion that all was not harmonious here.' He frowned.

'Unfortunately,' he said, 'matters have come to such a pass I fear this place is due to receive nation-wide prominence in the newspapers.'

'Poor Mr. Coltman,' Miss Frayle said. 'I can't help feeling sorry for him.'

'Everything he wished to avoid,' Inspector Pockett said, 'will explode around him with full force. Bad luck. Still at least he's alive and kicking, which is more than can be said for Elspeth Finch.' He turned to his sergeant. 'I think we'll leave Roy Allen till the last,' he said. 'Find out from the others what they know and build up the jig-saw from them. Perhaps then Roy Allen will be able to supply us with the vital pieces to tidy the whole thing up.'

He looked at Dr. Morelle for his agreement, and Dr. Morelle duly obliged.

'What you might call, to put it in a phrase: letting Allen sweat it out?' he said.

'Perhaps Miss Frayle could bring them here one by one,' Pockett said, 'since she knows them all?'

Miss Frayle crossed to the door. 'Whom do you wish to see first?'

'We'll start with Sullivan,' the inspector

said thoughtfully. 'Since he doesn't figure very much in yesterday's account.'

Miss Frayle hurried from the room.

'You won't mind if I stay, Inspector?' Dr. Morelle said smoothly. 'I will leave if you prefer it.'

Inspector Pockett smiled. 'I shall feel very much reinforced by your presence,' he said. 'In fact, I was about to ask you if you would remain, I'd appreciate your reaction to the answers I get from my questions.'

Gossiping groups of students gave Miss Frayle interested glances as she hurried in search of Sullivan. The news of Elspeth's death had evidently got around already, and obviously Willard, Isobel Ross and the others had found it impossible to try and get the classes working.

'The police?' Sullivan said when Miss Frayle found him in the gymnasium, aimlessly staring out of the window at the cold blue sky. 'Don't tell me I'm suspect Number One.'

'No, Mr. Sullivan, nothing like that,' Miss Frayle said in confusion. Then she realized that he was grinning at her and he wasn't taking it in the least seriously. 'Just a formality, you know. They'll be questioning everybody.'

His eyes were suddenly grave. 'Poor bitch,' he said. 'I can't say I liked Elspeth, but it's a shocking end. Is it murder, as rumour has it? Or did she do herself in for love of Roy?'

'I don't think it's really known,' Miss Frayle said cautiously.

He looked at her, nodding half to himself. 'That means it's murder,' he said. 'Bet old Hugo's shaken to the core.'

'Everybody seems to have got to know about it very quickly,' Miss Frayle said, as she accompanied Jeff Sullivan to the study.

'I expect whoever it was found her started the ball rolling,' Jeff said. 'Hugo came and told us just now that the cops were here, that Elspeth had met with an accident. Of course, the students living in town were full of it. Everyone's got a different yarn.'

Miss Frayle said nothing and then she was ushering him into the uncomfortable study. She did not wish to say anything that might spoil the impact of Inspector Pockett's questions.

Sullivan said something to Dr. Morelle who introduced him to the two detectives, as Sullivan was glancing round at them.

'I am a police officer, sir,' the Inspector said, 'investigating the circumstances of the death of one of your colleagues, Miss Elspeth Finch.'

'Is it murder?' Sullivan said as he sat down, and crossed one leg over another. His mood was still light and he appeared completely unimpressed by those facing him.

'All the indications point to that,' Inspector Pockett said. There was an air of reluctance about him, as if he did not enjoy having to admit the facts at this stage.

'Ask away,' Sullivan said, 'since I expect that's what you want me here for, and not to discuss the colour of my bright blue eyes. I'll answer your questions to the best of my ability, and,' he added, 'truthfully of course.'

Inspector Pockett shot him a glance

from under his grizzled brows. 'Thank you, Mr. Sullivan,' he said heavily. 'When did you last see Miss Finch?'

'Day before yesterday. That was Wednesday evening.'

'You didn't see her yesterday?'

'I never saw her at all yesterday,' Sullivan said quietly. 'Or if I did, I didn't notice that I had. I wasn't very much interested in the poor woman. She wasn't my type, and I don't think I was hers.'

'I'm not asking for speculations, Mr. Sullivan,' Pockett said.

Miss Frayle saw Sullivan look a little wary, as if he realized the mettle of the man he faced. He contrived to force an apologetic smile to his lips.

'I'd be grateful,' the detective said, 'for all the help you can give me. I want to build up a picture of Miss Finch's last hours of her life. Therefore, I'm interested in the movements of all who knew her and who might be able to throw any light on the matter.'

'I can't throw any light on her death,' Jeff Sullivan said. 'The news came to me as a complete shock.' He paused, looking round at the others. Then he braced his shoulders as if making an effort, his air of bravado was fast dropping away. 'Now what did I do yesterday?' he said. 'Here most of the time, took time out to go for a swim, that bathing-place in the river below the town.'

'What time was this?' Inspector Pockett said.

'Lunch time,' Sullivan said. 'I meant to have some food at that pub there. I was actually in the water when the storm broke, I remembered something about lightning being dangerous and hopped out quick. I sheltered in the old boathouse. I got dried and dressed, and just sat there watching the lightning and the rain.'

'You saw nobody you knew? Who else was sheltering in the boathouse?'

Sullivan shook his head. 'There were one or two people swimming when I got there, but they cleared off. Apart from them, the landlord of the pub can corroborate, if that's what you mean. I got a sandwich and a beer there after the storm blew over a bit.'

'And you left about what time?' Inspector Pockett said.

'Round about three, I suppose. It was after that, when I was walking back here, that I saw several people who knew me.' He half grinned. 'That's the best I can do for an alibi, I'm afraid.'

'I have not asked you for an alibi, Mr. Sullivan,' Pockett said smoothly. 'Thank you.' The detective turned to Miss Frayle. 'If you'd ask Mr. Willard to come and see me.'

Miss Frayle looked at Sullivan who stood up, she noted an expression of relief on his face under an air of nonchalance, and then she went out of the room.

She found Theodore Willard on the porch, staring at the police car.

'What is all this nonsense?' he said testily when Miss Frayle explained that he was wanted in the study. 'Elspeth Finch has been murdered or committed suicide, or whatever it is, and I'm very sorry about it. But I can't tell anyone anything.'

Nevertheless he accompanied Miss Frayle and in the study Inspector Pockett calmly repeated the statement he had made to Sullivan, and politely cut short Willard's complaints.

Willard pointedly ignored Dr. Morelle who remained in the background, a tall, angular silhouette against the window. Hopkins scowled at Willard's truculent manner.

'You can refuse to answer any questions I put to you, if you like, Mr. Willard,' the Inspector said affably. 'But you will realize that will not be very helpful to us and, frankly, we do rely on your help and that of everyone who can give us help in a case of this seriousness.'

Discomfited somewhat, Theodore Willard twitched his shoulders.

'What do you want to know?' he said. 'I'll tell you all I can.'

'When did you last see Elspeth Finch?' the Inspector said.

'God knows,' Willard said. 'Yesterday morning, I think, was the last time, or was it later?' He paused, as if trying to remember.

'You did not see her after the storm yesterday afternoon?' Inspector Pockett said, and Miss Frayle found herself looking at Willard, her hands clenched tensely.

'That's it, of course,' Willard said. 'I saw her on my way to town. I saw her meet up with Roy Allen. They went across the field together, towards Greenacre Woods.'

He broke off and looked at the detective-inspector, then Hopkins, then his gaze flickered on to Miss Frayle, then Dr. Morelle, and back to Pockett.

Inspector Pockett remained silent for a moment, while Willard's eyes flickered again over the others — the expression-less Dr. Morelle, Miss Frayle, whose glinting spectacles hid her eyes, and Detective-Sergeant Hopkins, who was studiously looking down at his notebook.

'I was a bit annoyed about it,' Willard said suddenly. 'I'd thought of walking to the woods myself. But I didn't want to meet either of them, so I continued along the road. I turned off at a pathway to the left of the road which brought me back to the Drama Workshop. I went slowly most of the time. After I got off the road on to the path.'

'What time was this?' Inspector Pockett said.

'I didn't know the time exactly, I don't carry a watch, but I got caught in the storm. I had no raincoat and got pretty wet before I ran into an old barn belonging to some farm. I saw the storm out there, and then came back here as fast as I could to dry myself. I took a class at four-thirty. There were enough witnesses of that, anyway.'

He looked at Inspector Pockett with an expression of surly triumph, which changed to one of puzzled annoyance as the detective gave him a fleeting smile.

'Thank you, Mr. Willard,' Pockett said mildly. 'That seems very clear, and you've been most helpful. If I have any further questions I would like to ask you I'd be glad if we could talk again.'

'Any time you like,' Willard said and hurried from the room.

After the door had closed on him Inspector Pockett looked at Miss Frayle. 'I gather he wasn't on good terms with Elspeth Finch?'

'I really can't say,' Miss Frayle said.

'Perhaps they snapped at each other a little, but they both had that kind of temperament. Besides Elspeth snapped at everyone.'

'Except you, I'm sure,' Pockett said.

Miss Frayle threw him a little smile. 'I got on all right with her,' she said. 'And, of course, there was Roy Allen, she never gave him the sharp edge of her tongue.'

'Isobel Ross and Roy Allen,' the Inspector said musingly. 'Shall it be the woman next? Miss Ross?' He rubbed his heavy jaw, then looked at Dr. Morelle and back at Miss Frayle.

'I tell you what, Miss Frayle,' he said. 'Let's change our mind, shall we? Would you be good enough to ask him along? Roy Allen, please.'

21

In the music-room, Roy Allen had been joined by Hugo Coltman, who had returned from his grim task at the mortuary in the town, and who had been rambling aimlessly around the Drama Workshop.

'It would be tragic,' Roy Allen was saying with intensity. 'I don't think you should give it up. I believe we should carry on with the end-of-term arrangements, in spite of everything. It may sound corny, but I believe in the idea that the show must go on.'

'I was only thinking of the place being filled with ghouls whose only thought would be of murder,' Coltman said.

'I don't see it like that at all,' the other said. 'I see it as a grand gesture to defy them all. Think of it, Mr. Coltman, you'd show them in London that you aren't defeated by all these incidents, that you're still the moving spirit behind a great and important part of our theatre.'

Hugo Coltman looked at him, his eyes glinting. His shoulders went back, and his chest swelled out.

He saw himself, a noble dignified figure, rising above the tragedy around him, out there on the stage of his theatre, accepting a storm of applause from his admirers. Hugo Coltman would not yield to defeat too easily, his Drama Workshop would defy the shafts of derision and tragedy.

'There is something in what you say,' he said in deep, warm tones. 'We will show them, eh? Yes, by heavens, we'll show them. Even if there will have to be some reorganization, anyway, with poor Elspeth Finch gone.' He took the other's hand and shook it. 'Splendid, splendid, dear boy,' he said. 'Thank you for your strength which has supported me in my moment of weakness.'

Roy Allen's eyes were shining. 'We'll have a performance you'll never forget, I'm sure of it.'

Miss Frayle's hesitant voice interrupted them.

'Mr. Allen, can you spare a moment, please?' she said politely. 'Inspector Pockett would like a few words with you.'

Roy Allen started, spinning round. 'The police? What do they want with me?'

'It is all right,' Hugo Coltman said reassuringly. 'Just a matter of some routine questions. They are checking on those who saw poor Elspeth yesterday.'

'I don't know anything about her death,' Allen said.

'I hope nobody here does,' Hugo Coltman said bitterly. 'But far better to let the police carry out their investigations their own way. You will find Inspector Pockett very pleasant and sympathetic.'

Roy Allen gave a shrug. 'If I can be of any help, of course, though I hate all the idea of questioning.'

He nodded to Hugo Coltman with a little smile, then he followed Miss Frayle to her office, his shoulders hunched. Coltman stood staring after him, his bold eyes narrowing speculatively.

Quickly assessing the nervous, highly-strung nature of the man Miss Frayle had brought into the study, Inspector Pockett repeated his opening gambit, introducing himself and his task there.

Roy Allen threw himself into a chair, sitting still rather hunched up, his face pale, a hand pushed under his jacket as if massaging above his heart. He grinned wryly.

'I've a devil of a lot on my mind, Inspector,' he said. He glanced at Dr. Morelle, still silent and brooding and aloof. 'Frankly I get a little het-up over any official stuff. Like having to go to the doctor, or the dentist.'

'The artistic temperament, sir,' Inspector Pockett said. 'We won't keep you long. You understand these are only one or two questions to which your answers may help us about this sad Miss Finch business.'

'Poor Elspeth,' Allen said softly. 'I didn't know her so very well. I saw her almost every day, of course, but no more than the other members of the staff here.'

'You were on reasonable terms, but not particularly friendly?' the Inspector said.

There was a little silence. The detective put the query casually enough. Miss Frayle caught her breath. Detective-Sergeant

Hopkins' pencil stopped, poised over his note-book, Dr. Morelle stirred slightly.

Roy Allen hesitated. 'I should say that lately, Elspeth — well, she seemed to have formed a great liking for me. I found it damned embarrassing.'

Inspector Pockett coughed gently. 'You mean, sir, she had fallen in love with you?'

Allen looked wryly at him, his mouth twisted in a faint, bitter smile. 'I gather you already know something of this, Inspector?'

'I don't want to upset your feelings, sir,' Pockett said, his tone full of understanding and sympathy. 'We don't have to go further into that, I'm sure.' The slightest pause, then: 'Did you see Miss Finch yesterday?'

'Yes, I did as a matter of fact. Unexpectedly. I found her waiting for me when I was out getting some fresh air. It was around lunch time. I was annoyed, quite frankly, I was turning over my work in my mind. Elspeth said she wanted to speak to me privately, and she was so insistent, that I agreed to go for a walk with her. At the back of my thoughts was that I had decided that I must tell her, once and for all, that there could be nothing between us.'

'Very awkward for you, I can see,' Pockett said gently.

'We walked towards the woods. She hadn't really got anything she wanted to say to me, nothing that I was the least bit interested in, anyway. I told her in a friendly way what I have told you, that I didn't care for her at all. There was rather a scene, I'm afraid.'

There was a tense silence in the room. But Roy Allen, if he sensed it, gave no sign. Miss Frayle could feel her finger-nails cutting into the palms of her hands.

Inspector Pockett gave a long-drawn-out sigh. 'So she took it badly?'

'Yes,' Allen said sombrely. 'I tried to make her realize how I felt, that it wasn't my fault I didn't — didn't reciprocate her feelings, but it was no use. So I left her, and turned back.'

'And this was where?'

'About half-way across the field. We'd stopped behind some tall bushes.'

Miss Frayle recalled how when she and Isobel Ross reached the gate, Roy Allen and Elspeth Finch were out of sight. What he was saying now fitted in with what she and Isobel had witnessed.

'I just kept on walking,' Allen was saying. 'I'm afraid I'd completely dismissed Elspeth from my mind. I was engrossed in this music of mine and the end-of-term show. I was so preoccupied that I walked right through the storm. I was absolutely soaking when I got back here. I went and had a hot bath and then went to my room.'

'And that was the last you saw of Elspeth Finch?' the detective said.

Roy Allen nodded. 'But other people must have seen her, after I left her, surely? If she headed for the woods, as apparently she did, she would almost certainly have met several people?'

'She certainly met someone,' the detective said grimly. 'After you left her, or while you were with her, you saw nobody else? Nobody you knew? Or anyone you didn't know?'

'I can't remember,' the other said. 'I

must have seen other people — none I knew, no — but I must have passed people. But I don't remember.' Suddenly he shuddered, his eyes haunted. 'If only to God I'd stayed with her, seen her to her home, this dreadful thing would never have happened.'

'Thank you for being so frank, sir,' Pockett said. 'I don't think I'll need to ask you any more questions at the moment.'

Roy Allen went out of the study. There was a short silence, then Inspector Pockett glanced at Dr. Morelle.

'What did you think of that?' he said.

'It would appear on the surface to fit in with what we already know from Miss Finch,' Dr. Morelle said. 'He spoke frankly, in fact, he seemed hardly aware of the gravity of his situation.' Dr. Morelle drew thoughtfully at his Le Sphinx. 'I have the impression,' he went on, 'he is not a physically strong man. Some heart complaint perhaps, though I may be wrong. But I noticed a bluish pallor about his lips, not that this is conclusive, of course. But from your point of view, Inspector, it might mean he was incapable of such a violent act as strangling.'

'There certainly was a hell of a struggle,' Inspector Pockett said.

'I was noticing his hands,' Detective-Sergeant Hopkins said, 'pretty strong fingers.'

'A musician's hands,' Dr. Morelle said, 'if he were playing the piano a great deal, would be strong. And Allen is of a wiry build.'

Inspector Pockett rubbed his chin reflectively. 'I'll pigeonhole your idea, Dr. Morelle,' he said. 'Many thanks. I must say it didn't occur to me that he looked anything other than a bit nervous and on edge. That, to my mind, accounted for his pallor. But if he's a sick man, as you say he may be, that may give us a new slant on him.'

Dr. Morelle tapped the ash off his cigarette, while Miss Frayle moved to the door, with a questioning look at the detective-inspector. He saw her move and nodded.

'Thanks, Miss Frayle,' he said. 'Miss Ross is the next on the list, if you would find her, please.'

22

'I'm Isobel Ross. I understand you wanted to see me?'

Isobel turned to smile at Dr. Morelle, before she faced the eyes in the heavy face which met hers, while a large hand indicated a chair.

Detective-Sergeant Hopkins flipped another page of his notebook and studied the tip of his pencil. Miss Frayle noticed that Isobel Ross appeared cool and firm, and it occurred to her that she took it all as lightly as Jeff Sullivan had apparently taken it.

'It's a dreadful business,' Isobel said. 'I can still hardly believe it. To think I saw her only yesterday, just before the storm. But I expect Miss Frayle has told you all about that?'

Was she mistaken, Miss Frayle wondered, or was Isobel Ross's tone just a little acid, as if she was hinting that Miss Frayle was some sort of police-snooper, who had rushed to tell Dr. Morelle and the detectives all she could, on learning of the murder? Miss Frayle blinked through her horn-rims and felt herself blushing.

'You saw her with Mr. Allen?' Pockett ignored Isobel's remark.

'Yes, I did. They went off across the field together, so far as I know.'

'And you didn't see her again, after that?'

'No, I didn't.'

'Not when you went out after the storm was over, Miss Ross?' Isobel threw a look at Miss Frayle, who blushed all over again. She thought of trying to explain that she had only done her duty in giving the police a complete picture of her own movements on the fatal day, and that she hadn't intended to sneak on Miss Ross. But she couldn't find the words, she could only squirm uncomfortably.

'No,' Isobel Ross said. 'The last I saw of her was when I was with Miss Frayle.'

'Perhaps you could tell me something about her, as a person. Did you like her?'

'No, I can't say I did.'

'Any particular reason?'

'I just disliked her.'

'Perhaps you'd tell me something about her which caused you to dislike her?'

Isobel shrugged. 'To be unkind, one might describe her as frustrated. Short-tempered, jealous, rather vicious. Definitely not agreeable.'

She saw the detective's eyes gleam, but she could not tell if it was because her succinct summing-up had amused him faintly.

'Jealous? Of anyone in particular?'

'Of any woman younger, more attractive or happier than herself.'

'Did you know of anyone who disliked her?'

'You mean anyone who disliked her more than I did. Disliked her enough to murder her?'

'I didn't say that, Miss Ross. I only asked you if you knew anyone who disliked her, actively, if you like.'

Isobel's voice was non-committal. 'I don't know. I don't think she got on too well with some of her students, but their views don't often get to our ears.'

Even as she said it, she knew it was

untrue, the students' feelings about the teachers almost invariably found their way back to the teachers, sooner or later.

She glanced at Dr. Morelle and she thought she detected a sceptical smile playing at the corner of his mouth. She wondered why she had taken the trouble to tell an unnecessary lie. Inspector Pockett seemed not to have noticed anything.

'How did the rest of the staff react to her?'

'I'd say we all found her a bit of a bore to get on with.'

'But you wouldn't say she had her knife into anyone specially?'

Tempted to startle him, Isobel smiled. 'Yes, me. She couldn't stand me.'

But all she got was a faint gasp from Miss Frayle, her attempt at humour passed the big, square-shaped detective by. 'And you reciprocated her feelings?'

She frowned, suddenly impatient. 'I told you so. But if you mean did I hate her enough to want to kill her, the answer's no.'

'Of course, of course,' Inspector Pockett said and waved a vague hand. 'I simply have to find out all I can about her, nothing personal about all this, I can assure you, Miss Ross.'

Her retort was cynical. 'I suppose you're questioning us all, one by one, and then you check up to see where our stories about each other differ? Entertaining for you, I shouldn't wonder, but rather a waste of our time.'

He merely nodded apologetically and said placidly:

'I'm sure all this must be very upsetting for you, I know you're in the thick of your end-of-term work.'

His reasonableness only made her answer more unreasonably, and she flared up. 'We've certainly had enough distraction lately. Already one of my students — '

In mid-sentence she stopped speaking, as if someone had struck her. Pockett's whole attitude changed, he leaned forward.

'What is it? What is the matter?'

Isobel's eyes widened. 'Where did — did it happen? Greenacre Woods. It was Greenacre Woods, wasn't it?'

'Why, Miss Ross?' Miss Frayle said.

'Have you thought of something?'

Isobel Ross saw the detective's gaze boring into her. She saw the gaunt shadow of Dr. Morelle looming up at her.

Brian Wickham, she thought. Now it'll all have to come out that I saw you in the blessed woods. My God, how can that be explained away?

She sighed. 'I went out after the storm, I went along the lane at the back of the woods,' Isobel Ross said.

'That was after the storm was over, you say?' Inspector Pockett said, and made a move towards her. She nodded and he went on.

'You saw no sign of Miss Finch?'

'No.'

'Who did you meet?'

For all that she was expecting it, the question made her tense. She clasped her hands. The Inspector did not miss the movement.

'I met Brian Wickham,' she said. 'One of my special students; we walked part of the way back together. Then he went on home. He lives in the town.'

Now it came, the question she dreaded

most of all. She braced herself.

'Where had this student come from? The same way as you?'

'I don't know exactly,' she said. 'I didn't ask him. I was so surprised to see him there at all. He'd been walking in the woods, he told me.'

'I see,' the detective said. He glanced at Hopkins, then at Dr. Morelle. 'How old is he, Miss Ross?'

'He's seventeen. He lives with his mother. They're not well off. He's by far the cleverest student in the Workshop.'

'I'm sure,' Inspector Pockett said. 'I expect I'll be having a chat with him, in due course.'

'Before you do that, let me explain about him,' Isobel said.

The other stared. 'What is there to explain? I only want to ask him where he was before and during the storm.'

She shook her head wearily. 'He's a bit nervy, especially just at the moment when he's got the end-of-term show. It's a big chance for him, he's been working so hard, slogging away, perhaps he's over-done it.' She swung round upon Dr.

Morelle. 'Isn't that right, Doctor?'

Dr. Morelle had stepped forward. 'I've already had a talk with Miss Ross about the young man,' he said to the detective. 'I'd say he sounds as if he is suffering from a certain amount of nervous strain, not unusual in a type of his temperament.'

'I understand that, Doctor,' said Inspector Pockett, 'but Miss Ross makes me think he may have something on his mind he's scared to talk about.' He turned back to Isobel. 'If you know what it is and you're shielding him — '

'It's not that.' She knew a blinding frustration. 'You know we've had a lot of trouble here lately, and I think it's got on his nerves. I really believe it's begun to affect his memory, and that for an actor is the end. I'm afraid if you talk to him, it may only upset him even more. After all, I have his future to think of.'

The detective scratched his moustache doubtfully. Dr. Morelle turned to him.

'If I may make a suggestion? I'll have a chat with Wickham and elicit all I can from him about what he may have seen or knows about while he was in the woods.'

Pockett nodded quickly. 'That's fine, Dr. Morelle,' he said. 'I'll leave him to you.'

'Thank you, Dr. Morelle,' Isobel Ross said. To Inspector Pockett she went on: 'I'm sure he knows nothing, but if there is anything he can tell you, he will, I know, with Dr. Morelle's help.'

It was the end of the detective's interview with Isobel Ross, and after she had gone Inspector Pockett raised an eyebrow at Dr. Morelle.

'She's a big woman herself,' he said, 'and she didn't like Miss Finch very much.' He sighed heavily.

Miss Frayle began to feel her heart pounding. Dr. Morelle said slowly: 'Strangling is not a woman's way of setting about a murder.'

'I know,' Pockett said. 'I've never come across it in my experience.'

'There always has to be a first time,' Detective-Sergeant Hopkins said.

Inspector Pockett glanced at him, then pursed his lips. 'She is a strong-looking woman,' he said, 'no getting away from it.

227

I wouldn't like to have to struggle with her myself.'

'I don't know that I'd altogether mind,' Hopkins said. The smirk on his good-looking face faded before Pockett's admonishing frown.

'Dr. Morelle,' Miss Frayle said suddenly, 'I've just had an idea about Isobel Ross.'

'Go on,' Dr. Morelle said encouragingly, 'and tell us, Miss Frayle.'

'She said how she met Brian Wickham in an awful state,' Miss Frayle said. 'But I wondered — I know this sounds ghastly — but couldn't it be the other way round? Supposing that what Inspector Pockett suspects is true, and that she did strangle Elspeth Finch — oh, it does sound dreadful, but I'm thinking of Brian Wickham — supposing he came on her suddenly, and was so shocked that he had this blackout thing?'

Miss Frayle's voice trailed away as she glanced at Dr. Morelle and saw that his chin was sunk broodingly on his chest.

'I should have thought that if that had happened,' Detective-Sergeant Hopkins said, 'she'd have done him in as well to quieten him.'

'She might have banked on Wickham's memory,' Inspector Pockett said. 'She knows more about him than most people, she'd be able to size up the situation and what the chances were of him suddenly remembering what he'd seen. But then why should she kill Elspeth Finch anyway?'

Inspector Pockett breathed in deeply, swelling his chest with an expression of frustration, and exhaled through pursed lips.

'If your theory was to hold water, Miss Frayle,' Dr. Morelle said, 'that Isobel Ross had murdered Miss Finch, then surely you yourself must have been a witness of the crime? Did you not say you accompanied her back here after you saw Miss Finch go off with Roy Allen?'

Miss Frayle wished for the floor to open and swallow her up as she realized how utterly stupid her theory had turned out to be.

'You saw Isobel Ross again immediately after the storm had ceased,' Dr. Morelle said, 'setting out for the walk during which she was to encounter Brian Wickham. She did not appear to have gone out in the storm, did she?' Miss Frayle shook her head. 'Then,' Dr. Morelle said, 'how could she have committed the crime?'

'I'm afraid I hadn't thought of all that,' Miss Frayle said weakly. I wish I hadn't thought such a dreadful thing about Isobel Ross, she told herself fervently. It just serves me right, though I was only thinking she was trying to put it on to young Wickham.

'It seems to me,' Inspector Pockett said, 'that of all those we've questioned Miss Ross has the best alibi of the lot for the time after Roy Allen left Elspeth Finch, at least she seems to have been with Miss Frayle, and, under the circumstances, what better company?'

Dr. Morelle gave a quiet laugh. Miss Frayle regarded him miserably, then she realized he was not smiling at her altogether unkindly, but rather as if she was on equal terms with him in this sinister business and they were sharing a quiet joke together. She brightened appreciably.

'Have you any suggestions, Doctor?' Inspector Pockett was saying.

'The earlier incidents anyway,' Dr. Morelle said, 'if not Elspeth Finch's murder, have their basis somewhere in the pasts of Hugo Coltman and at least one other person here. That photograph, for instance. I should imagine that inquiries into the histories of those concerned with Coltman about the time that photograph was taken might prove fruitful.'

'Agreed,' Pockett said. 'You can leave that to us. And I'll leave it to you, Dr. Morelle, to see what you can get out of Brian Wickham.'

23

As Isobel Ross went through the hall in the direction of the common-room, a figure in a sports jacket came through the front door, saw her and grinned, then raised something in his hands. Before she could protest there was a flash of magnesium. The man grinned again.

'Miss Ross, aren't you? It was you who met the student when he came out of the woods. And what about your views on the murder? Any idea who killed Miss Finch?'

She was furious. 'No, I haven't,' she said. 'Who've you been talking to?'

'People in the town,' he said. He waved his camera.

'You'd better not let Mr. Coltman see you,' she said. 'He'll smash that to bits.' She stared at him. 'You mean people in the town know about Brian Wickham? How could they? Who could have told them?'

'Perhaps he did, or his family, or his

friends,' he said. He grinned at her again, as she began urging him towards the front door. She was scared that Hugo Coltman would appear. There would be a frightful scene, she knew, if he found that the newspapermen were already on the scent.

'The C.I.D. boys are here, are they?' He was on the porch steps looking at the police car. He glanced at the Duesenberg. 'Who does that vintage job belong to — Hugo Coltman?'

'If you really are interested,' Isobel said. 'That happens to belong to Dr. Morelle.'

'For Pete's sake,' he said, 'have they called him in? That gives the story a bit of colour all right. The old maestro himself on the job. And what about that secretary of his, Miss Frayle?'

'She's here, too, naturally,' Isobel said. She wondered what the other would say if he knew that Miss Frayle was hardly a stranger to the Workshop. 'Now if only you'll put their photos in the paper, that would be much more sensible of you. I'm sure you've got dozens of pictures of them, and besides they're news, surely. I'm not.'

He grimaced. 'You'll be news yourself, all right, before this is all over,' he said. 'For Pete's sake, if you have a murder in the house, you must expect a bit of publicity.'

Isobel's look was withering. She turned on her heel, but his voice stopped her.

'I tell you what,' he said. 'I'll let you off if you'll give me a line on Miss Finch which I can pass on to my paper. You know, personal angle stuff. You must have known her pretty well. What motive could anyone have had for killing her?'

'Perhaps she was as nosy as you're being,' Isobel said. 'And somebody did to her what I hope somebody will do to you.'

And with that she left him, and went off quickly to the common-room, angry with herself that she had behaved with such a lack of dignity towards the horrid little man, and yet pleased about the choice of words of her reply.

She found them all in the common-room. Theodore Willard, Jeff Sullivan and Roy Allen. Suddenly she looked at them and finding herself unconsciously seeking Elspeth Finch's sharp-eyed, olive face, she realized what her death meant. No more that acid-tongue, that slim, vital figure, that frustrated personality. Isobel experienced a sense of loss and it came to her as a shock.

'How did you make out?' Jeff Sullivan said.

'All right,' she said, lightly.

It was Willard who told her that Coltman had decided that all students should call it a day until Monday. Monday, which began the week and culminated in the end-of-term show.

She thought of Brian Wickham, what a mess-up for him all this business was. She tried to make herself believe that this ghastly tragedy which had struck the Drama Workshop was not more important than Wickham and his career. All the same she was thankful to learn that work wouldn't start up again until next Monday, it would give everyone a chance for a breather.

'Has he any theories?' Roy Allen said, lighting a fresh cigarette from the one he had just finished.

'He's hardly had a chance yet,' Sullivan

said. 'Though now he's finished grilling us, the action will start. What's his angle, Isobel?'

She shrugged. 'He's trying to build up a picture of her life, her habits, her friends, enemies and so on.'

'Enemies?' Roy Allen said. 'Are we to suppose she had any? Is he trying to make something of the fact that she wasn't popular here? Don't tell me he's got one of us lined up as the murderer?'

Isobel looked at him curiously. 'Who do you imagine killed her then, Roy? I'll stake my bet it was somebody connected with this school.'

There was a sudden silence, then Roy Allen said:

'I should say she met some man who tried to get off with her, and came to a sticky end defending herself from a fate worse than death.'

'No, I can't believe that,' Jeff Sullivan said. 'This was no unexpected meeting the poor thing had with some madman. I think she tumbled to the identity of whoever it was had been causing the high jinks we've been having here, and she threatened to give him away.'

'You mean she was trying to blackmail him?' Theodore Willard said. He considered the idea for a moment. 'I suppose that is more likely to be the answer.'

Isobel pushed a strand of hair back from her brow and sighed. 'Has Hugo come up with any ideas about it yet?'

Sullivan shook his head. 'It's completely knocked him flat,' he said. 'When I heard about it first I thought it was some hideous kind of joke, I think most of us did.' He turned to Roy Allen. 'You were the only one who took it calmly.'

Roy Allen stammered. 'I was as much taken aback as anybody. I suppose I was so preoccupied with my music, the penny didn't drop at first.'

'Are the detectives concerning themselves with all the other pranks, too?' Willard said to Isobel.

'Inspector Pockett didn't tackle me about it,' she said. 'But I've no doubt he got the full story out of Dr. Morelle and Miss Frayle.'

'What sort of a part is Dr. Morelle playing in this grim little charade?' Jeff

Sullivan said. 'He's one of those pools who run deep. Hardly said a word while I was in there, just stood in the background, like some dark eagle sizing up his prey, before pouncing.'

'You're mixing your metaphors a bit,' Willard said. 'But I agree, he's not exactly a cosy type.'

'I rather take to him,' Isobel said.

'Even supposing Miss Finch had known who the joker was,' Willard said, 'and had been blackmailing him, it still seems a drastic way of silencing her. I mean, he wouldn't have got into such serious trouble even if she had given the game away.'

'Not even for cracking young Bennett's skull open?' Sullivan said. 'I don't know if you'd care to face the police about that, but anyway I'd say it'd ruin your career. Apart from which the man — or woman — is presumably potty. The only thing is, if it is the explanation I can't think why Elspeth was such a fool to take the risk.'

'There's something odd about that,' Isobel said. 'She was shrewd enough, generally. She must have felt very sure of herself.'

Miss Frayle came into the room, looking untidy and worried.

'How's it all going, Miss Frayle?' Isobel said to her.

'Inspector Pockett and Detective-Sergeant Hopkins have left,' Miss Frayle said. 'And Dr. Morelle has seen Mr. Coltman and gone off to talk to Brian Wickham.'

'What's he got to do with it?' Roy Allen said.

'My star student is now the star witness, or even star suspect,' Isobel Ross said. 'That damned detective thinks he had something to do with the murder, or at least that he saw something suspicious when he was in the woods yesterday afternoon.'

Roy Allen stared at her incredulously. 'You don't really mean he thinks Wickham actually saw the murder?'

'Perfectly true,' Isobel Ross said. 'From what Wickham said, it sounded as if he was there at the same time Finch was being strangled.'

'And you had to tell the police this,'

Sullivan said to her.

'I opened my big mouth too wide,' Isobel said bitterly.

'But Isobel,' Roy Allen said, 'did he see anything of it? The murder, I mean?' He sounded excited.

'Yes,' Theodore Willard said, frowning in bewilderment, 'either he did see something, or he didn't.'

'You know that Wickham's in a pretty jumpy state,' Isobel said. 'The commotion of the past week hasn't improved matters for him. First, it was just a dry-up or two, but when I met him yesterday, he'd been wandering around trying to pull himself together, he said. But he admitted that he had very little recollection of what he'd been doing, just a vague memory of stumbling about among trees.'

'Blackouts,' Jeff Sullivan said, 'when he doesn't know what he's doing?'

Miss Frayle saw Sullivan's face tauten as he moved towards Isobel Ross. Then he turned from her and spoke to the others.

'It's pretty obvious to me,' he said,

'that this is the answer to the whole thing. Nobody in his senses would have attacked Elspeth, but a half-crazed student might have set on her. I'm not surprised Inspector Pockett's so interested.'

Isobel Ross could hardly control her anger. For a moment Miss Frayle thought she was going to smack Sullivan across his face.

'Don't talk rubbish,' she said. 'Wickham had no more to do with it than I did.' She turned to Miss Frayle. 'Thank God it's Dr. Morelle who's going to handle him,' she said. 'And not that lumbering policeman, who'd have driven the poor boy off his rocker.'

'I'm sure Dr. Morelle would be glad to know how you feel about him,' Miss Frayle said.

'You can't expect much else from a policeman,' Willard said. 'He couldn't care less about the artistic temperament.'

Sullivan crossed to Isobel Ross and put his hand lightly on her arm, and she smiled at him. Willard went over to the cupboard and dragged some play-manuscripts from a shelf. It seemed to Miss Frayle that he handled them roughly. One of the scripts slid to the floor, scattering some loose pages.

'Damnation,' Willard swore viciously, then bent to pick up the fallen sheets.

Miss Frayle, bending to help him, retrieved an open envelope from under the table. It was an envelope for tickets to the Old Vic. She thought there were some tickets inside it, but Willard took the envelope from her and pushed it into his pocket.

Isobel was looking at Willard. Had Inspector Pockett said anything to him about seeing Elspeth and Roy Allen together, she wondered. She must remember to ask Miss Frayle, and then she asked herself what did it matter? If Willard had seen anyone else in the vicinity of the murder he would have said so.

What a tangled web it all was, she thought, looking round at the others. Jeff Sullivan, Roy Allen, Theodore Willard. Did they know more than they pretended? Or was Inspector Pockett entirely on the wrong track?

Or, she found herself wondering, in a despairing panic, had he been nearer to the solution of the mystery when he had picked on what she had blurted out about Brian Wickham?

24

The editor of the *Gazette* looked up. 'Hullo, Miss Frayle. Have you brought Dr. Morelle with you?' He got up and gave her a chair, as she shook her head.

'I've come along on his behalf,' she said.

'Would it be about the murder, Miss Frayle?'

'Not exactly, and yet it may be,' Miss Frayle fancied she sounded as enigmatic as Dr. Morelle himself.

The fat, bald man tilted his chair back and grinned.

'Anything I can do to help Dr. Morelle,' he said.

'He thought you might have something in your files about an incident that happened in 1935. Dr. Morelle thought you might have filed it, you see, because Hugo Coltman was involved.'

The other's eyes narrowed with concentration. ''35? What was that, I wonder?'

'It was a trial,' Miss Frayle said,

watching him. 'A man was prosecuted for misappropriation of money belonging to Mr. Coltman when he was acting at a theatre up in the North.'

'That does ring a bell,' and the chair came down with a crash. 'The Wilson case. I remember it now, a nasty business.' He looked at her oddly. 'Why on earth are you interested? Should have thought that business was never mentioned at the Workshop. I know Coltman hated Wilson for stealing the money. At least that's what they said, otherwise he'd have hushed it up.' The *Gazette* editor shook his head. 'But perhaps it wasn't entirely Coltman's fault. Wilson was Coltman's manager, and he had the handling of the money at the box-office. He behaved more like a fool than a criminal.' He shrugged his shoulders. 'Anyway he went up before the beak, and got two years. It's said that Coltman didn't help the case, but after all Wilson had robbed him, betrayed a position of trust, and all the rest of it.'

'And weren't there any extenuating circumstances?'

'In the opinion of many people, yes. Wilson had a wife and ailing son to support, and the fact that he'd lost his job and would find it hard to get another might have been considered punishment enough in itself.'

'Do you know what happened to him when he came out?'

'I've no idea. May I ask why Dr. Morelle is so interested?'

Miss Frayle could not have answered the question. Apparently some inspired notion on Dr. Morelle's part which was connected with the disappearance of the photograph from the frame in Hugo Coltman's study.

Miss Frayle failed to see what all this had to do with Elspeth Finch's murder. True, Elspeth had been looking at the picture, and been very interested in it. There must be some link between the photograph and the Wilson case, but where did the murder come in?

The editor was watching her curiously. Miss Frayle gave him an uncertain smile.

'You know about the unpleasantness at the Workshop before the murder, I mean?'

The other grinned wryly. 'I got an earful over the phone for printing that stuff. I suppose I ought to have realized at the start that Coltman isn't the sort to offer a story like that to a newspaper, but at the time I never doubted it was him.' He looked at her quizzically. 'I suppose he didn't find out who it was?'

'No,' Miss Frayle said. 'But perhaps Dr. Morelle can see some connection between Miss Finch's death and the other affair.'

The editor got to his feet and led the way to a room stacked with filed copies of the *Gazette*. A little sandy-haired man greeted him and Miss Frayle.

'Miss Frayle, from the Drama Workshop, wants to read up the Wilson trial. I expect we've got something on it on account of Coltman being featured in it.'

The man's eyes widened. 'The file's already dusted off,' he said. 'You're the second within the past week or so. What's the attraction?'

The other man spun round. 'What do you mean? Who else has been round here?'

'She didn't tell me her name,' the sandy-haired man said. 'Just said she came from the Drama Workshop. It was last week she came in, Friday, it must've been.'

'What did she look like?' Miss Frayle said. 'Can you describe her?'

'I didn't take much notice of her, I was pretty busy at the time, but I'd put her about thirtyish. Bit on the short side. Dark haired, slim, gave me the impression she'd been a dancer.'

Miss Frayle stared at him. 'Elspeth Finch,' she said. 'Dr. Morelle was right then, there is some connection. We've got to find it.'

'Do the police know you've come round here?' the editor said. 'Or what Dr. Morelle is up to?'

'They will,' Miss Frayle said. 'Don't worry. You won't get into trouble for letting me find out all I can here.'

'That's all right. I don't want them thinking I've been holding out on them over this stuff.'

He was thumbing through the 1935 file. When he came to March he stopped and gestured towards the faded headline, Miss Frayle drew nearer, then caught her breath.

'Theft of Box-office Takings. Theatre Manager Arrested.

'Robert Wilson, Hugo Coltman's General Manager was arrested at his hotel last night, charged with misappropriating money belonging to Mr. Coltman, whose company is playing at the Royal Theatre this week. Wilson, when arrested, pleaded that extreme hardship had driven him to this means of obtaining money, and asked for lenient treatment in view of his having a wife and delicate son to support. It was, he said, to pay for treatment of his son that he had been tempted to take the money.'

'There's another clipping here,' the editor said. Miss Frayle lifted the yellowing sheet of paper, to be confronted by a photograph of Hugo Coltman, severe, handsome, in astrakhan-collared overcoat and black, wide-brimmed hat, his head tilted back in the defiant poise she knew so well.

He must have been a striking figure on

the stage, she thought, though was there, she wondered, even then something chilling about him, a lack of sympathy, a proud loneliness that must have obtruded between himself and his audiences, and in his private life, cut him off from friendly contacts? She recalled never having heard of any women where Hugo Coltman was concerned, he had never married.

Or had there been, she suddenly thought, something about a young actress he had married early in his career, who had, a little while later, run off with another actor and gone to America?

Underneath the photograph were paragraphs reporting the evidence he had given at the trial. Quickly she scanned it, and as she did so her heart sank. What a harsh and pitiless condemnation.

'A flagrant breach of trust ... despicable form of theft ... robbing his fellow-actors of their salaries ... ' As she read the phrases she could picture him there in the witness box, even if not exactly enjoying the experience unable to resist giving a performance, demonstrating his command of the scene to the court, packed to see him in an unusual rôle. Miss Frayle had, in her mind's eye, a picture too of the figure in the dock.

'What a fool he must have been,' she said. 'Mr. Coltman I mean. An unfeeling, dehumanized, pompous mountebank — Hadn't he any appreciation of why poor Wilson took the money?'

The editor regarded her quizzically, then ran one finger along the dusty paper.

'I suppose to him the point was that Wilson had stolen the money that belongs to the great Hugo Coltman, he had betrayed the great Hugo's trust. There was no excuse, no mitigation for such an action.'

'Is there a photograph of Wilson anywhere?' Miss Frayle said. The man beside her turned another page and she found herself looking at what had obviously been a personal snapshot, showing Wilson in open-necked shirt and flannels, laughing into the camera.

She bent her head closer, then looked up in annoyance.

'It's dreadfully blurred, you can't see his features at all. Is there a better one anywhere?'

251

The other flipped through the file again, but no further photos came to light. Miss Frayle looked worried.

'Dr. Morelle's convinced there's some link between Wilson's trial and this present business. I wish someone knew what had happened to him after he came out of prison. It was a two-year sentence, that means he'd have been released in 1937.'

'Probably got remission of sentence which would get him out a bit earlier,' the editor said. He frowned to himself. 'I seem to remember something about that,' he went on. 'We've always been interested in the case, as I've said, because of Coltman setting up his place here. I think one of the reporters got hold of something about Wilson. Wait here. I'll find out.'

He lumbered off and disappeared into the reporters' room. Miss Frayle knew a sudden stirring of hope. She began to read the account of the trial again. It was extraordinary how Hugo Coltman's intolerance blazed from the fading print of the clippings, as he gave his evidence.

It was when the judge passed sentence that Wilson's nerve had broken. The report showed that throughout the trial he had maintained a quiet calm, as he heard the doom-laden words of the judge he had stood dazed, unbelieving, then he had spread his hands in a helpless gesture.

'But my wife and child? What's to happen to them?'

Miss Frayle found herself picturing him, his question unanswered, hanging in the still air of the court. Wilson had looked out across the sea of faces to where Hugo Coltman sat, and in a voice that broke hysterically he had shouted abuse at him.

'This is your doing. You wanted me punished, damn you, you wanted me to go to jail. I'll pay you back for it one day. I swear I will.'

And struggling and shouting he had been dragged from the dock. With a long sigh Miss Frayle raised her head as the editor returned, chewing on his pipe.

'He wasn't exactly a model prisoner to start with,' he said. 'Then he became silent and moody, sank into a lethargy and hardly seemed to be aware of where he was, or why he had been sent there. Towards the end of 1936 he went down with pneumonia, he showed no will to recover and in November of that year he died.'

Miss Frayle made a queer, strangled sound.

'He died? Good heavens, then Dr. Morelle's been on the wrong trail altogether. He'll be absolutely infuriated.' She bit her lips with disappointment. 'I'm sorry to have given you all this trouble. It looks as though I've been wasting your time.'

'Aren't you forgetting something, Miss Frayle?' the other said. 'How about Miss Finch? If she came round here looking up the case,' he jabbed his pipe at the newspaper-cuttings, 'must be a tie-up somewhere.'

Miss Frayle gasped. 'I'd forgotten about her. I do believe you're right, there must be something in it. But where?'

'You might do worse than let Dr. Morelle worry over that,' the editor said. 'He's bound to come up with the answer.'

25

While Miss Frayle had been active at the *Gazette* offices, Dr. Morelle had been left by Brian Wickham's mother, a thin, wispy woman, with Brian in the comfortable little sitting-room of the small villa, set in a row in a quiet street.

'The news about Dicky Bennett continues to be good,' Dr. Morelle said, and Wickham's features relaxed. 'So that you need feel no further anxiety on that score.' He did not mention that Bennett had been unable to provide any more information other than that which had already been given about his assailant in the dark theatre. 'How is it with you?' Dr. Morelle went on. 'Any more blank patches since yesterday?'

'No, Doctor, but I keep feeling a bit foggy.'

'You don't feel that you might remember more about what happened to you in the woods, if I tried to prompt you?'

'I don't know. I've tried to prompt myself.'

'As an actor, you must know that to try to prompt yourself is difficult. Don't you always get someone to hear you in your part, give you the cue?'

Brian Wickham nodded, smiling a little. 'I've never dried up in my part like this,' he said. 'I can't help feeling that something did happen while I was there. I've been struggling to remember what it was, but I don't know what.'

'Do you think you saw someone there?'

'I don't know,' he said. 'I just can't explain. But don't you ever get that feeling, a sort of oppression, that there's something you've forgotten; something you meant to say or do? It's like that with me over this, as near as I can describe it.'

'I understand perfectly,' Dr. Morelle said. He gazed round at the photos of actors on the walls, including several of Coltman. He glanced at the titles of the books on the shelves. Theatre text-books, plays and famous actors' and actresses' biographies. 'I suggest you don't work too hard at remembering. Allow your mind to relax and this thing will come drifting up into your consciousness.'

He began to talk, at first generally, of the theatre; then in more detail Dr. Morelle began sketching in the supreme personalities of Shakespeare's plays, he related them to the glittering sordid scheming adventures of Elizabethan politics, the princes and the captains. Brian Wickham sat wide-eyed at the depths of knowledge which Dr. Morelle plumbed; and then when he talked of the theatre of to-day, of the motion pictures, television, soon question and answer flew back and forth between them.

Mrs. Wickham opened the door at tea-time. Dr. Morelle saw the anxious look she fastened on her son, and that look changed to surprised pleasure, as she found him relaxed and the tenseness gone, a little colour had crept back into his face, and his expression seemed more hopeful.

Presently Dr. Morelle was at the wheel of the Duesenberg driving through the late afternoon in the direction of the Drama Workshop. He turned into the drive, and the car wheels crunched to a halt at the porch steps. There was the black police car, and then he heard a rush of footsteps across the hall and Miss Frayle appeared on the porch, and ran down the steps. She informed him somewhat unnecessarily that Pockett had called with Detective-Sergeant Hopkins. Even while he was getting out of the car she was, characteristically, giving him an account of her discoveries at the *Gazette* offices.

When she had ended, Dr. Morelle lit a Le Sphinx, and leaned casually against the yellow car door. 'The pieces of the jigsaw are beginning to fit into place,' he said. 'Soon the picture will be complete.'

'Picture of what?' said Miss Frayle.

'A portrait of the murderer,' Dr. Morelle said. He drew at his cigarette, to glance up as Pockett and the young detective-sergeant appeared out of the hall.

'Thought I heard your car,' Inspector Pockett said. 'I've been chatting to Mr. Coltman, I wanted to check some information I have.' He indicated one or two pieces of paper he was carrying. 'You've heard of this idea of his of going through with his end-of-term show next week?'

'He mentioned it to me, yes,' Dr. Morelle said. He glanced at Miss Frayle. 'No doubt Miss Frayle, when she has time off from the activities upon which she's engaged for me, is already seeing to the final preparations.'

'All the plans are well in hand,' Miss Frayle said.

'I'm not sure it's a good idea,' Inspector Pockett said.

'I don't see what should go amiss, Inspector. In fact the end-of-term show had appeared to me as a means, perhaps, of inducing a certain person to come out into the open.'

'The madman?' Detective-Sergeant Hopkins said, while Miss Frayle stared at Dr. Morelle.

Dr. Morelle shrugged. 'Who knows? If he and the joker are one and the same, next Friday's performance might seem to him — or her — to be an ideal opportunity for another damaging blow at

Hugo Coltman. This time, I am sure you will be well prepared for any eventuality.'

Inspector Pockett nodded. 'You can take it from me there will be a few of us around, just in case.' He handed the papers he was holding to Dr. Morelle. They were typewritten sheets. 'Some notes about the people here,' he said. 'I'd like you to glance at them.'

Dr. Morelle read through the papers.

Theodore Willard: Date of Birth: 12.1.11. Education: Hart's Secondary School, Preston. Manchester University. Became interested in amateur dramatics at University. Gained professional acting experience and studied elocution at Spode's Academy of Drama. Toured abroad and Great Britain with professional companies, and later set up as a private tutor. 1939-42 Naval Service. Joined Hugo Coltman Drama Workshop 1943 after six months in hospital for war injuries. Unmarried.

'His University career seemed to show no great academic attainment,' Dr. Morelle said. 'While the same may be said of his stage career.'

He glanced at the next sheet of paper. Jeffrey Sullivan: born 9.11.15. Dublin Grammar School. New College, Oxford. B.A. Hons., French and German. Foreign Correspondent, *Daily Standard*, London and Berlin, 1938-39 travelled in Near East and North Africa and Mediterranean countries generally. 1939 Royal Artillery. Two years' service to rank of Major, 1941 invalided out. 1941-44 Fleet Street and freelance, army fencing champion, 1940. Joined Coltman 1945. Unmarried.

'Something of a rolling stone,' Dr. Morelle said. 'A seeker after excitement and variety?' He shrugged. 'The out-of-the-rut quality of his job here must have attracted him.'

Dr. Morelle turned the page. Isobel Hilda Ross. Born February 1925. Educated Lewes and Oxford. B.A. Attracted by stage and joined repertory company. Took teacher's diploma, at intervals taught in private schools. Joined Coltman's Drama Workshop 1949. Unmarried.

Dr. Morelle stared meditatively at the paper, surrounded by a cloud of cigarette smoke which curled lazily on the calm air. 'Surprising she hasn't married,' he mused, then he said: 'She seems to have had considerable experience as a teacher.'

'She disliked Miss Finch, all right,' Pockett said ruminatively.

Dr. Morelle nodded thoughtfully. 'But real hatred? Would she have killed? Is she even the sort of person who'd play all those stupid tricks?'

Dr. Morelle turned to the next page of typewritten notes. Roy Henry Allen: Date of Birth: 9.10.28. Longmore's Junior School, Streatham, then private tutors. Joined music-publishing firm, studied Royal Academy of Music, piano and organ, also composition. Exempted war service: forces entertainment, radio engagements. 1946-48 teaching. Joined Hugo Coltman Drama Workshop 1949.

Inspector Pockett took the notes from Dr. Morelle. 'What do they amount to?' he said. 'Bare facts don't give you much.'

'Background, personality, that is what tells the story,' Dr. Morelle said. 'The photograph, I feel certain, is a positive link.' He told the detective the result of

Miss Frayle's inquiry at the *Gazette*.

Pockett glanced at Hopkins, and pursed his lips. 'If only Wilson hadn't died,' he said, 'then the idea that was beginning to form in my mind . . . ' He broke off and turned to Dr. Morelle. 'I was trying to work out if anyone at the Drama Workshop could have been George Wilson. Disguised, perhaps, or with a change of name. But it didn't fit, anyway, and now it's scotched entirely. It's no good thinking Wilson is at the back of this. In fact it's what you might call a dead end, Dr. Morelle.'

'I am not unconvinced that there may be a link with this past case,' Dr. Morelle said. 'And if Elspeth Finch discovered what it was, we must find it. There is still scope for inquiries along those lines.'

'We'll work on it,' Inspector Pockett said, but Miss Frayle thought there was not a great deal of enthusiasm in his tone. 'How about the Wickham kid?' he said.

'That's a tricky situation,' Dr. Morelle said. 'I've spent the last two or three hours with him, and I think I can claim that he will talk, but when exactly I can't tell you. Tomorrow? The next day?' Dr. Morelle shook his head. 'And when he does tell me what he saw, we don't know what it will amount to.' Dr. Morelle paused reflectively. 'All the same,' he said, 'it seems to me that I ought to have warned Isobel Ross to keep silent to the others about her encounter with Wickham.'

'Too late,' Miss Frayle said, 'she told them all about it in the common-room. I was there and heard her before I went down to the *Gazette*.'

Dr. Morelle frowned at the tip of his cigarette. 'A pity,' he said.

'What's on your mind?' Detective-Inspector Pockett said.

'Yes, why?' Miss Frayle said.

Dr. Morelle looked first at the detective, and then at Miss Frayle. 'I was under the impression,' he said, 'that you believed the guilty person to be one of the teachers here? If that is the case doesn't it occur to you that they might have been present when Isobel Ross recounted the story, and that the murderer might then consider Brian Wickham a potential danger?

Suppose his memory returns and he remembers the details of that afternoon, he may even have actually witnessed the murder in Greenacre Woods? That would be a trifle disconcerting for the criminal, wouldn't it?'

'You mean Brian Wickham may be in some form of danger?' Inspector Pockett said.

'I merely ask you to put yourself in the position of the killer.' He turned to Miss Frayle. 'What action, for example, would you take, Miss Frayle?'

His voice was quiet, unemphatic. She shivered, her mouth went dry.

'Whoever it is, is in our midst,' Dr. Morelle said. 'If and when Brian Wickham's memory comes back, he may tell us of what he saw yesterday afternoon at about the time Elspeth Finch was murdered. He may be able to point a finger at the guilty person.'

26

Dr. Morelle meditatively paced the drive outside the Drama Workshop. It was a cool dusk, with the sky tending to be overcast. A bat flew in dipping circles above. He could hear the muffled clacking of Miss Frayle's typewriter, late in her office, and he was waiting for her to join him.

He had not forgotten the ulterior motive which had prompted him to accept Hugo Coltman's invitation to come down from London to investigate the Drama Workshop mystery. Events had taken a much more dramatic turn than had been foreseen, but Dr. Morelle did not intend to lose sight of his original idea of luring Miss Frayle back into his employ.

He paused, turning to look back at the roofs and chimneys of the house, silhouetted against the sunset sky.

Was Hugo Coltman, that man of

quicksilver moods arrogant and tyrannical, to be the victim of yet another assault upon his pride and endeavour in his Drama Workshop within the next twenty-four hours?

It was Thursday evening, to-morrow was the day of the end-of-term show. Ten days had passed since the place had been shaken by the murder of Elspeth Finch, and fear and suspicion had haunted the Drama Workshop. On the surface, at any rate, there had been no further developments in the case.

The inquest, in the small bare room in the magistrates' court in the town, had been formal and quickly disposed of.

The Coroner, a brisk, bespectacled little lawyer, had kept the proceedings moving quickly: formal identification of the body had been made by Hugo Coltman; medical evidence as to the state of the body and the cause of death; the police evidence had been given. Evidence had been taken from members of the Drama Workshop staff concerning when and where they had last seen Elspeth Finch alive.

An attempt made by a juror to bring up the matter of the previous unpleasantness at the Workshop, now common knowledge in the town, had been politely but firmly sidetracked by the Coroner. They were there to decide the cause and circumstances of Elspeth Finch's death, there was no evidence that this had any connection with the other incidents, Miss Elspeth Finch had not died at the Drama Workshop.

The inquest had ended with the verdict that Elspeth Finch had been murdered by a person or persons unknown.

For the Drama Workshop it had been days of turmoil. Elspeth Finch's murder had brought nation-wide prominence in the newspapers. The telephone had rung incessantly, with inquiries from the Press. Hugo Coltman had kept Miss Frayle dealing with requests from students' parents. Was it safe to leave their sons and daughters there? All these dreadful happenings.

But all the students had stayed on, with the end-of-term show slowly beginning to force the gossip and rumour engendered by Elspeth Finch's death out of the picture. The show must go on, had become the watchword. One steadying influence had been the presence of the eminent Dr. Morelle upon the scene. The newspapers had fastened upon him with typical alacrity and brashness.

'Any statement to make, Dr. Morelle?'

'Naturally I am shocked at Elspeth Finch's brutal killing.'

'Any idea who might have murdered her?'

'Were such knowledge in my possession I should hardly waste my time acquainting you of it, I should have passed it on to the police.'

'Any line you can give us about the Finch woman's past?'

'Your own newspaper files should be able to provide you with all the information about her past career.'

'Seems to have been some funny happenings here before the murder, Dr. Morelle. Can you tell us anything about them?'

'The actions of this mysterious practical joker were malicious and despicable; I don't think Hugo Coltman saw in them any cause for amusement.'

'You haven't an inkling or suspicion who this joker is? Somebody with a vicious grudge against Coltman?'

'You may read a more detailed report in the local paper,' Dr. Morelle had smiled disarmingly, 'whose morbid and ghoulish interest in matters which don't concern it, is second only to that of the more widely read newspapers.'

Strolling quietly up and down Dr. Morelle allowed his mind to review the events that had occurred since Miss Frayle had sent for him on Hugo Coltman's behalf to come down to the Drama Workshop. He went over the personalities of those who might be involved, their actions, their evidence given to Inspector Pockett and at the inquest, at which he had been present.

In his imagination he followed the paths that had brought them to their present taut and nervous existence, the shadow of recent dramatic events looming over them.

Back in the house Miss Frayle typed

that last word of the last item of work for the evening, and got up from her desk. She took off her spectacles, blinked and then a little smile appeared on her face. She was looking forward to dinner with Dr. Morelle.

She gave a startled jump as the telephone rang.

'Could I speak to Dr. Morelle?' It was a man's voice, it seemed to be muffled.

'Who wants him?'

'He doesn't know me, but I know he's investigating the murder of this woman. I've got some news which may interest him.'

'Will you hold on, please?'

Miss Frayle put the receiver on the desk. She stood hesitantly. Should she trouble Dr. Morelle with what was probably only some hoaxer? Then she hurried across the hall to the front door. From the top of the porch steps she saw Dr. Morelle's dark figure moving slowly against the trees overhanging the drive. She called out to him, and he looked up, approaching her as he did so.

'Someone on the telephone for you.'

'Who is it?'

'It's a man, but he won't give his name. He's got some news for you about the murder, he says.'

Dr. Morelle's smile was faintly mocking as he glanced up at her from the foot of the steps.

It suddenly occurred to her that it was because he was thinking that she rather enjoyed these mysterious little incidents such as anonymous phone calls, with which she had become not unfamiliar when she had been working with him. Her suspicion that this was what was going through his mind was proved to be correct, for he said to her:

'Quite like old times, isn't it, Miss Frayle? Is our mysterious voice holding on?'

'I told him to,' she said. 'Shall I tell him you're not here?'

For answer he came up the steps, and brushed past her into the hall. She followed him, the hall was shadowy now in the fading light. In her office Dr. Morelle picked up the receiver.

'Hallo?' he glanced at Miss Frayle questioningly.

'Who is it?' she said.

'Since no one's here,' he said, 'I can't answer your question.' He spoke into the mouth-piece again. 'Hallo?' He turned to her with a faint shrug. 'You are sure it was someone, Miss Frayle?' he said. 'And that your febrile imagination hasn't been running riot?'

She threw him a look of protest. 'Of course it was someone,' she said. She moved forward as he offered her the receiver, and she spoke into it. 'Hallo?'

There was no answer, but she turned to Dr. Morelle with a triumphant look. 'I'm surprised at you, Doctor,' she said. 'Obviously it was somebody, because they haven't rung off. You can tell by the sound at the other end. They've left the receiver off the hook.'

His lean face lit up with a glimmer of a smile. 'Thank you, Miss Frayle,' he said, 'for pointing it out to me.'

She was not sure that he was mocking her or not, as he took the receiver from her and listened, his eyes narrowed speculatively. A shiver ran down Miss Frayle's spine as she watched him.

'Who could it have been?' she said, 'and why have they gone away? It was a man, I'm sure of that,' she went on frowning, 'though his voice was muffled as if he were trying to disguise it.'

'Did he sound as if he was aware I was here?'

She hesitated. Then she said: 'Yes, he did. He did sound as if he knew you were here all the time.'

He nodded. 'From which we may deduce that it was someone with whom we are acquainted.' It seemed to her he was about to say something else, then he changed his mind and paused for a moment. 'You say he said he had some news about the murder?'

'Yes,' she said.

Dr. Morelle waited for a few more moments with the receiver to his ear, but nothing happened, and he hung up. 'No doubt, if it is anything of any importance,' he said, 'our mysterious caller will phone again.'

Miss Frayle eyed the telephone as if expecting it to ring into life once more, but it remained silent. Dr. Morelle moved towards the door and looked across the hall. He turned back to her and said:

'I have no intention of waiting all night while he makes up his mind. Ready, Miss Frayle?'

It was growing dark as they went out to the Duesenberg.

They turned out of the drive and headed along the road in the direction of the town. Dr. Morelle's profile was brooding and then suddenly he stopped the car. Miss Frayle eyed him with surprise. They had proceeded only about thirty yards along the road from the drive.

Then she saw as he got out of the car that he had stopped beside a telephone-box. She watched him as he opened the door. What on earth could he be doing, making a phone call? Why hadn't he used the phone in her office, or waited a few minutes until he got to the hotel?

Dr. Morelle did not go into the phone-box, however. From where he was he could see in the gloom the receiver hanging from its flex and the sound of the dialling tone as it swung there gently.

He hung it up and let the door slam

back heavily and stood staring into the half-light beyond the phone-box and across a field. The Drama Workshop made a dark, irregular mass silhouetted against a clouded sky which merged into a purplish-black on the horizon. Then he turned and got back into the car.

The Duesenberg moved forward again, its powerful lamps cutting the night. Miss Frayle said to the sombre profile beside her:

'What was it?'

'The answer to the phone call,' he said. 'Whoever made that call did so from that call-box.' She stared at him completely at a loss as he went on:

'Whoever it was knew I was outside the house, and that the chances were I should come in to answer it. They couldn't have phoned me from the house, so where did the call originate? It was seeing the telephone-box that gave me the idea. What one might call a sudden intuition. They left the receiver off.' He must have glimpsed the somewhat smug smile that crossed her face. 'You must not imagine that you have a monopoly of moments of instinctive knowledge,' he said, from the side of his mouth.

She blinked at him in the darkness, his saturnine face caught the greenish glow from the dashboard-lights, she only half understood the explanation he had offered her for the mysterious phone call, as she said:

'Who was he? And why should he want to attract your attention?'

Dr. Morelle said musingly: 'That was the nearest phone they could get to.'

'You mean it was someone in the house, who deliberately went out to get you to the telephone in my office?' She stared at him blankly.

He nodded.

'But whatever for?'

He gave no reply. She puzzled furiously, trying to fathom what could possibly be behind the strange action of the unknown caller. It appeared obvious to her that Dr. Morelle was correct in his deduction, that the call had come from the call-box.

She remembered an occasion several months ago when as a result of a storm all the telephones in the Drama Workshop had failed to work, and while the matter was being put right, everyone had used the phone-box on the side of the road. It had meant a few minutes' walk through a little copse and across the field to the opening in the hedge on the side of the road.

She mentioned this now to Dr. Morelle and added: 'That means that it was someone at the Workshop, and we know it was a man.'

'If it was, as seems likely, someone on the staff,' he said, 'it is not necessarily conclusive that it was a man's voice you heard.' And answering her unspoken question he went on: 'Isobel Ross, for instance, an experienced voice teacher, would, I fancy, find little difficulty in disguising her voice. You said it sounded muffled, as if it was disguised.'

They had reached the crest of a hill which dipped down towards the town, and she stared ahead following the beam of the headlights. It was a fast stretch of road, needing care because of the sharp bend where the road levelled out just before forking, one way by-passing the town, the other leading to it.

Dr. Morelle pressed the brake-pedal, to ease up the speed a little. There was no response to his pressure, and instinctively he pressed harder. He felt the palms of his hands moisten slightly as he gripped the wheel. The brake-pedal felt spongy to his foot, he felt nothing of the hard grip of the brake linings.

Again he pressed hard down, trying to pump the brake, but the car rushed on, gathering speed, even though he had taken his foot off the accelerator.

'The brakes,' Miss Frayle's voice rose as she realized that something was wrong.

She heard an exclamation from Dr. Morelle. Staring ahead in horror, as the car rocketed down the hill, she saw the lights of another car coming round the bend, and shining dazzlingly as the oncoming vehicle came on to the straight stretch before the hill.

Panic-stricken, she turned her head away, there was a squeal as Dr. Morelle, missing the oncoming car by a coat of paint, began pulling at the hand-brake. It failed to grip, then she heard a snapping sound.

The connection had broken under the strain. Swaying and zigzagging, the car sped onwards, and Miss Frayle heard herself screaming.

In that moment Dr. Morelle pulled the steering-wheel round and the car shot across a patch of grass at the side of the road, as with his other hand he switched off the ignition.

The car bounced across the rough grass, beginning to be slowed down by the heavy ground. Then it fell into a ditch, and it lurched over and stopped with a jarring thud. Miss Frayle's head struck the door and she fell sideways, stunned, as Dr. Morelle was flung against her.

Miss Frayle lay there for a moment, her senses swimming up sickeningly out of swirling mists. The night air was cool on her face. She was lying outside the car, which was still half in the ditch, and Dr. Morelle knelt beside her, looking at her anxiously in the reflected light of the still glowing headlamps.

'Dr. Morelle,' she gasped painfully. 'You're — you're all right.'

'Slightly shaken,' he said, 'but fortunately I was not thrown against the windscreen. The shock was felt on the side of the car. How do you feel?'

'A little bit sick,' she groaned, 'and my head aches terribly.'

Dr. Morelle helped her to her feet as a man ran to them over the rough ground.

'Thank heavens you're all right,' the newcomer, a short thick-set man, said. 'I saw you coming down the hill, and — '

'The brakes failed,' Dr. Morelle said. 'Luckily I saw this stretch of grass by the road, and took the only chance there seemed to be of slowing the car down. A case of that, or a crash at the bend.'

'Perhaps I can take you somewhere,' the man said. 'My car's just over there,' he waved an arm in the direction of the road. 'I was coming along behind you.'

'Thank you,' Miss Frayle said warmly. 'We're going to the Lamb and Flag.'

'I think first,' Dr. Morelle said quietly, 'if you'd drop us at the police station.'

The man glanced at him sharply, but

said nothing. Miss Frayle felt Dr. Morelle's arm round her shoulders, and was comforted by it. Dr. Morelle switched off the Duesenberg's lights and then the three of them made their way towards the stranger's car.

'Unusual for hydraulic brakes to fail like that,' the man said, as they reached his car, a medium-sized saloon.

'I was thinking somewhat along similar lines,' Dr. Morelle said. But he said no more.

It so happened that Inspector Pockett was in the office at the police station and he looked up with some surprise as Dr. Morelle, and Miss Frayle, her face still white and strained, her glasses askew, walked in accompanied by the sergeant on duty.

'Something happened?' Pockett said. He saw Miss Frayle's face as she slumped into a chair. 'What's going on?'

Dr. Morelle's eyes narrowed as he stared back at the detective. He lit a Le Sphinx, slowly dragging at it, and Miss Frayle noticed that the fingers that held his cigarette were steady as if their near escape from a horrifying death was a matter of daily routine to him.

'I have a strong impression, Inspector,' Dr. Morelle said, through a cloud of cigarette smoke, 'that an attempt has been made to murder Miss Frayle and me.'

'Good God,' the Inspector said. 'How? What the devil happened?'

'If you send your experts to look at the Duesenberg,' Dr. Morelle said, 'I think they will confirm what I am about to tell you.'

He told Pockett where the car was to be found, and the detective went out of the office to give the necessary instructions. While he was away the duty sergeant reappeared with cups of strong tea. Miss Frayle sipped hers gratefully.

Inspector Pockett returned and Dr. Morelle began telling him of the mysterious phone call Miss Frayle had received, how no one had been at the other end, and then his intuition which had caused him to stop at the roadside call-box.

'It will appear obvious to you,' Dr. Morelle said, 'that the phone call was a subterfuge to get me out of sight of my car, while whoever it was made it got back from the call-box and tampered with the brake.'

Inspector Pockett nodded grimly. 'Damned sorry you've struck this, Doctor,' he said, and gave Miss Frayle a sympathetic smile. 'We'll know something about what was done to your brakes very soon, meanwhile I'll arrange for a car to take you to the hotel.'

When the detective came back into the office, a police driver accompanied him. Miss Frayle, the colour back in her face, turned to him expectantly.

'Not much damage, sir,' the police driver said to Dr. Morelle. 'It's towed here now, and we'll soon get it going again. I spotted what caused the brakes to fail.'

'Yes?' Pockett said.

'Master cylinder containing the brake fluid had a pipe disconnected, and was partly emptied of fluid, probably before the car started out,' the other said. 'During the few times you used the brakes before coming to the hill, the rest of the fluid was pumped out by the action of the brake. There was nothing left when you needed it most. No brake pressure at all.'

'A cool, skilful attempt,' Dr. Morelle said sombrely. 'The culprit calculated that the car would be so badly damaged in the smash-up that the tampering with the brake-cylinder would not be noticed. Verdict: accidental death, and Miss Frayle and myself neatly out of the way.'

He paused, dragged deeply at his Le Sphinx, his eyes hooded. Then he said: 'Thank you for looking after us, Inspector. I intended telephoning you to-night from my hotel in conjunction with Brian Wickham. While he is much more relaxed, I have advised him not to attempt to appear at the performance to-morrow. Everything has been arranged with Isobel Ross and Coltman, and Wickham will not suffer. He will continue on at the Workshop and be given every chance next term to make up for all that has held him back. He is remaining in the security of his own home, his memory so far as the afternoon in which you and I were most interested has not improved. I may decide to induce a return of memory by hypnosis.' He paused: 'But somehow I fancy that it may not be necessary.'

'Why is that?' Inspector Pockett said.

'To-morrow will produce a climax to this business,' Dr. Morelle said. He glanced at Miss Frayle with a little smile. 'My intuition, shall we say, warns me.'

Miss Frayle noticed that his smile was blank and humourless, and her flesh crept as she recalled her and Dr. Morelle's narrow escape. Would Elspeth Finch's murderer be there at the Drama Workshop end-of-term per-formance to-morrow, hidden behind a mask of innocence?

27

Nervously Miss Frayle glanced round, all the time half expecting something dreadful to happen, setting the audience into a turmoil.

It was early afternoon. So far the Friday had passed without untoward incident. Before lunch, stage and film personalities, stars, producers and playwrights had arrived; students' parents, relatives and friends; and the students themselves, some silent, some laughing and joking too loudly, according to their temperaments, as they prepared for the various scenes they were to act.

A murmur of conversation had broken out in the theatre as one of the pieces, the Forum Scene from Julius Caesar, ended to a long rattle of applause. Newspaper reporters were making one or two notes, their expressions bored. Few of them had come to watch Hugo Coltman's Drama Workshop end-of-term performance. They were there to savour the atmosphere of death and suspicion which filled the air.

During the morning Miss Frayle had been in the common-room, checking through final arrangements. Willard, Isobel Ross, and Jeff Sullivan had been there. Isobel had been expressing her acute disappointment that Brian Wickham was not going to appear, and Sullivan had been commiserating with her.

Hugo Coltman had looked in for a moment to speak to Miss Frayle. He had been cheerful, exuberant almost, reassuring Isobel Ross that her star pupil would get another chance to show his quality next term; chatting about the weather, and apparently full of optimism about what the day would bring, he seemed to have no doubt that it would be a day of triumph for the Hugo Coltman Drama Workshop.

After he had hurried out, Miss Frayle had heard Isobel say to Jeff Sullivan:

'Wish I felt as chirpy. I think he's taking an awful risk. Say something dreadful happens again with every top theatre and film big-wig present?'

Sullivan shrugged, his eyes thoughtful. 'What can happen?' he said, and seemed indifferent to the whole thing.

'I don't know,' Isobel said slowly. 'I can't imagine what Dr. Morelle or the police are doing, allowing it all.'

'Maybe the search for Elspeth's killer has shifted away from the Workshop. That's the sleuths' main preoccupation, after all. More important to them than the possible antics of another joker.'

Roy Allen had drifted in absent-mindedly, a big folder containing his music inevitably under his arm. He was edgy and nervous, pale-faced, as Miss Frayle greeted him, and wished him good luck.

As she went out Miss Frayle spoke cheerfully to Theodore Willard, pacing restlessly before the windows overlooking the garden, warm in the sunshine and bright with flowers.

'I think Hugo's crazy,' he said truculently, speaking to Miss Frayle as well as the others. 'Allowing these people to come rubber-necking through the place.

Does he imagine they have come to watch the performance? They're ghouls, morbid-minded ghouls, the lot of them.'

Miss Frayle had not waited to hear the rest of it. In the hall she had seen Hugo Coltman greeting newspaper reporters, being affable with them, and photographers who had begun to swarm everywhere, mingling with the visitors.

Now Miss Frayle glanced at Dr. Morelle beside her, an unopened programme in his hand. He was silent and remote, as if his thoughts were far away from the murmur all around him, the svelte, beautiful women, the sophisticated men, the aroma of cigars and expensive perfume. She recalled that he had become more brooding after he had gone back-stage, Miss Frayle accompanying him, just before the curtain had gone up on the first scene of the show.

They had met Roy Allen, and Dr. Morelle had wished him good luck for his musical contribution. Allen had done his best to appear polite, but Miss Frayle thought his nerves were at snapping point. Then he had been called away by the stage-manager about some point concerning the grouping of his singers, and he had absent-mindedly placed the music folder he had been clutching on to a nearby chair. It had slipped off as he dodged around a flat to reach the stage, and Miss Frayle picked it up.

It was open at a page: Chant for Youthful voices. The words danced in front of her eyes. With casual fingers she had flicked the pages.

'Voice Line and Piano — Sopranos and Contraltos only,' she had read.

She thumbed through the score, staring short-sightedly at the words written below the melodic line:

What shall we sing, we children?
Love, praise for this place . . . is that what we feel?

She shook her head at what seemed to be a jumble of phrases, and turned a page.

There must be an end . . .
To greed and falsehood,
Fickle hearts and evil ways . . .

Then the contraltos' theme:

> We children dedicate our lives,
> Our youth . . .

A bit bizarre, Miss Frayle thought, maybe uncomfortable, but she knew nothing about this sort of thing.

Dr. Morelle had stood beside her.

'What's this, his composition?' he had said. And she thought he had seemed to tense as he glimpsed the page she had been reading.

Then they had heard Roy Allen shouting for his music, and quickly Miss Frayle had closed the score and ran with it to him. He had taken it from her as if he could not believe he had left it behind. As if he had let go of it as a result of some mental aberration.

The moment had arrived. The orchestra ended the intermission music and the theatre darkened. Miss Frayle could feel the palms of her hands moisten as she looked at the dark profile beside her. Was Dr. Morelle suddenly feeling as she did, that something momentous was about to happen? What had made him seem so withdrawn since that encounter backstage with Roy Allen? Or was she imagining it all?

The curtain rose, and a spotlight caught Roy Allen, standing by the gleaming grand piano. About him outside the pool of light that held him were grouped his students, formally dressed; the young men in dark suits, the girls in skirts and blouses. Programmes rustled as the audience looked to see what item this was in the programme.

Roy Allen looked amazingly young and intense, his face pale, severe in its concentration.

'Ladies and gentlemen,' he said, his voice barely carrying to his listeners, 'this afternoon I am about to conduct a work which has never been heard before. By this I do not mean just that it has not been performed in public, but that nobody, not even my students who've been rehearsing it, have heard it in its entirety. I have called this work Chant for Youthful Voices,' he went on, his voice strengthening. 'It expresses all that I feel for the Drama Workshop, my hopes for it; for those who work and study here. Ladies and gentlemen, 'Chant for Youthful Voices.''

He bowed and sat at the piano, and as he struck the first chords Miss Frayle glanced at Dr. Morelle, and her heart jumped as she saw that his former withdrawn expression had been replaced by an intent stare. And suddenly she heard him whisper to himself: 'All that he feels for the Drama Workshop, his hopes for it.'

Three harsh chords from the stage, then a soaring of voices; sopranos, high and thin:

'What should we sing, we children?

'What should we sing?'

The deeper voices of the young men, slow and thoughtful, holding the last word:

'Love, praise for this place . . . ?'

'No, no more,' cried the sopranos, and in a flare of sound, 'Hatred,' flung out the contraltos. Then again, stronger, more defiant, the same words:

'What should we sing, we children?

'What should we sing?'

'Love, praise for this place . . . ?

'No, no more. Hatred.'

And the voices faded on a wailing echo. Half the audience sat straighter. Half the faces mirrored bewilderment; others, still unconscious of what was going on, stared blankly at the singers.

Roy Allen shifted out of one key into another, sharper, harder, and the voices crept in with an uneasy rhythm. Sopranos followed him up, in a rising scale, while contraltos hammered out a harsh throbbing dissonance, atonal, discordant. Only the thoroughness of his teaching kept them together, the magnetism of his concentration at the keyboard. Miss Frayle could see his lips mouthing the words. Separately, the voice lines had seemed odd, with unusual harmonies, queer changes of key. Together, welded with the capering accompaniment into one whole, the monstrosity of what Roy Allen had written became manifest. This music was hideous; a blatant blare one moment, a sliding ugly fall the next. Sopranos, wavering higher and higher, made a shrill challenge while the contraltos, ignoring, triumphing, swung from key into key, weaving a strange pattern of their own, parodying, mocking.

'There must be an end . . . ' began the sopranos.

'We children dedicate our lives,

'Our youth . . . ' interrupted the baritones.

'To greed and falsehood,' finished the girls.

Miss Frayle saw Dr. Morelle out of the corner of her eye, rigid in his chair. She glanced across at Hugo Coltman, his mouth slack, his whole expression showing his shock and horror. Some among the audience were looking at him, wondering what he would do.

Staring up at Roy Allen, his shoulders heaving, his head thrown back, his strong hands crashing on the keyboard, she knew then that they had found Hugo Coltman's crazy tormentor, and, the dread thought struck her, Elspeth Finch's murderer.

Hugo Coltman half rose. The youths finished their line.

'. . . to these, admirable traits.'

'Fickle hearts,' the girls sang triumphantly, 'and evil ways . . .'

'Admirable traits,' the baritones repeated, and Roy Allen turned, his face twisted in a smile, to the audience. The singers might have a growing realization of what they were doing, yet they found themselves desperately unable to call a halt as the music throbbed and soared.

'No praise . . .' it was a whisper from the girls.

'To God,' from the boys, capping their phrase.

'To us, the struggle and the shame,' went on the girls, their meaning blasphemously distorted by the youths' interjection.

'We suffer . . .' in a wail of agony from the contraltos.

'And he laughs to see . . . laughs to see,' affirmed the sopranos in a rising scream of sound.

'A weeping and a tortured frame,' flung out the boys.

The music was reaching its climax, in a frenzy of chromatics the students swept again through their suddenly horrible words, by their expressions terrified themselves, but caught helplessly in the cataract of sound.

'No praise to God?

'To us the struggle and the shame,

'We suffer, and he laughs to see

'A weeping eye and tortured frame.'

Allen was swaying at the piano, his hands darting through the intricacies of the accompaniment.

Hugo Coltman in the front row of the stalls leaped to his feet.

'Stop,' he yelled hoarsely. 'End this foul nonsense.'

With a whirl of notes, a final sickening sweep of voices, it was over. Roy Allen crashed his hands on the keys, in a shattering discord.

He stood up, bowing mockingly, his pale face creased in a devilish grin. Then the curtain fell, the house-lights came on and the orchestra somehow managed to slide into some innocuous interval music.

Dr. Morelle pushed Miss Frayle to her feet as the audience, some of them standing up, began talking, incredulous and appalled. 'We gave him the opportunity and he's taken it,' he said sharply.

Breathlessly, Miss Frayle chased after him as he went through the little pass door at the side of the proscenium. With a look over her shoulder she saw Hugo Coltman, his face an ashen, distorted mask, in the centre of a commiserating group.

Dr. Morelle with Miss Frayle close on his heels hurried on to the stage, in time to see Inspector Pockett, with a grim-faced Detective-Sergeant Hopkins beside him, facing Roy Allen, behind the students, looked bewildered and embarrassed.

'Roy Henry Wilson, commonly known as Roy Allen,' Inspector Pockett was saying, 'I have a warrant here for your arrest on a charge of murdering Elspeth Finch. It is my duty to warn you that anything you say will be taken down and may be used in evidence.'

28

Roy Allen's face, a bluish tinge round his lips and nostrils, was working with horror. He looked uncomprehendingly beyond the two detectives at Dr. Morelle and Miss Frayle as they paused on the stage.

'Murder?' His eyes blazed. 'I didn't murder Elspeth Finch. I swear it. You're wrong. Insanely wrong.'

'You will have every chance of answering the charge,' Inspector Pockett said. 'There may be further charges of causing grievous bodily harm to Richard Bennett, and of the attempted murder of Dr. Morelle and Miss Frayle.'

'You fool,' the other's voice rose to a scream. 'I didn't kill her, I tell you. Yes, I accidentally hurt Richard Bennett. I was responsible for all the trouble, the slashed pictures, the fire — but I'm not a murderer. Nor did I try to murder Dr. Morelle or anyone else.'

Inspector Pockett and Hopkins made a

move towards him, and with an animal grunt of fear and anger, Roy Allen twisted round, he turned racing off the stage.

'Stop him,' yelled Inspector Pockett and, with Hopkins beside him, went after Allen.

Following them raced Dr. Morelle and Miss Frayle, her eyes wide, a hand holding her glasses to her nose. They heard the thudding of feet as Roy Allen dashed up the stairs past the dressing-rooms, then they heard the crash of a door.

'He's gone out on to the balcony,' Miss Frayle said. Ahead of them as they gained the top passage, the two detectives had thrown themselves at the door at the end of the passage and hurled it open.

In the corner of the balcony, in the bright sunshine, Roy Allen half crouched.

'Keep away, damn you. I hated Hugo Coltman, he killed my father, I hated him and everything he stood for.' The words poured out in an insane rush. 'Keep away, or I'll throw myself over. I mean it — '

Inspector Pockett and Detective-Sergeant

Hopkins stood there breathing heavily, indecisive.

'I've ruined his damned Drama Workshop,' Roy Allen was gasping triumphantly, then his gasps became a sudden moan. He clutched at his chest, his fingers clawing at his jacket. Inspector Pockett and Hopkins ran forward. Miss Frayle cried out as she saw Roy Allen's contorted face, the grin of pain. Then he swayed and fell.

Dr. Morelle was beside him in an instant.

'My God,' Inspector Pockett said, as he saw Dr. Morelle's expression. 'He's dead.'

Birds sang, the scent of flowers hung sweetly on the sunlit air. There were footsteps behind her and Miss Frayle spun round to meet the glances of Hugo Coltman and newspaper reporters and photographers. She turned back to the scene before her as Dr. Morelle gravely examined the inert figure at his feet. He looked up and nodded to Pockett.

'Perhaps it was the best way out,' the detective said. 'Poor devil was obviously out of his mind.'

Some time later, when the shocked throng had gone, and the ambulance had taken Roy Allen's body away, and the place seemed strangely quiet and deserted, Dr. Morelle and Miss Frayle, Inspector Pockett and Hopkins, together with Hugo Coltman went into Miss Frayle's office.

Hugo Coltman had finished his long moan about how he he was now utterly ruined and he would have to close the Drama Workshop, finally and for ever. His listeners had heard him patiently and done their best to persuade him that the Hugo Coltman Drama Workshop was not in fact finished, but would rise Phoenix-like from the ashes of disaster and sudden death.

'I don't mind betting you, sir,' Inspector Pockett said, 'that you'll be opening up again next term, sure as eggs.'

Hugo Coltman looked only half convinced as the detective turned to Dr. Morelle. 'What about the staff?' he said. 'I'd like a word with them to thank them for the co-operation, and all the rest of it.'

'They all went into the town,' Miss

303

Frayle said. 'They had friends down from London, and they went with them. Drinks at the Lamb and Flag, I suppose.'

'Never mind,' Pockett said, 'I don't suppose it'll worry them if they never see me again.'

Hugo Coltman muttered something about suffering from a blinding headache and went away in search of some aspirins, leaving Dr. Morelle and Miss Frayle, together with Hopkins and Pockett, who, rubbing a thick finger along his moustache, said musingly:

'I suppose it was Elspeth Finch's infatuation for Allen proved her undoing. She got on to him and spotted that 'School For Scandal' photo and realized his resemblance to George Wilson. It was she who discovered he'd changed his name.'

'Blackmail?' Detective-Sergeant Hopkins said.

Pockett nodded. 'Let's say she tried to make him — um — kinder to her. She grew more persistent, he told her to do her worst, there was a furious quarrel — '

'So he murdered her,' Miss Frayle

whispered. 'What is so odd,' she said, 'was that I never recognized his voice, that time I overheard him with Elspeth in the garden, or when he asked for Dr. Morelle over the phone.'

Dr. Morelle had remained very silent while the others had been talking, drawing reflectively at his Le Sphinx. Now Inspector Pockett glanced at him curiously as Miss Frayle went on: 'I can't think those two voices were the same, even though I barely heard the first, and the one over the phone was muffled.' She looked at the others, but no one had any comment to make.

Inspector Pockett was still eyeing Dr. Morelle, a faint shadow of unease beginning to move across his face. 'It's not exactly a tidy ending,' he said with an effort at lightness, 'far from it, from a police point of view.' He broke off and said to Dr. Morelle: 'Suppose you'll be going back to London to-night, Doctor?'

'I shall not be leaving just yet,' Dr. Morelle said. He added: 'The unpleasant-ness that brought me down here is ended,' and there was a tone in his voice that brought everyone's gaze on him. 'But your case, Inspector,' he went on, 'is not yet closed.'

Inspector Pockett's head jutted forward, as if he could not believe his ears.

'What are you driving at, Doctor?' he said.

'I mean Roy Allen didn't murder Elspeth Finch, her murderer still goes free.'

Inspector Pockett continued to stare at Dr. Morelle in stupefaction.

Miss Frayle and the detective-sergeant moved closer to him, a feeling of tension suddenly tautened the atmosphere of the office.

'The photograph,' Dr. Morelle said. 'The fact that the photograph was still in Miss Finch's handbag when she was found dead. If Roy Allen had murdered her because she knew who he was, the last thing he would have done would have been to leave it in her bag. He would have destroyed it, and with it all chance of anybody linking him with his father.'

Inspector Pockett opened his mouth and started to say something, but Dr.

Morelle interrupted him.

'Elspeth Finch's murderer,' Dr. Morelle said, 'did not know she possessed this photograph, did not know why she had taken it, did not know she had a hold over Allen on account of it. He was unaware that the photograph was of any importance at all. No, Elspeth Finch was murdered for an entirely different motive.'

'But what?' Inspector Pockett said.

Dr. Morelle's gaze flickered over Miss Frayle. 'You overheard her talking to a man,' he said to her. 'You heard her telling him that it was all over between them.' Miss Frayle nodded, a chill of fear and excitement overwhelming her, as the conversation she had heard in the garden came back to her.

'That could be your motive,' Dr. Morelle said, turning to Pockett. 'That unknown man could be your murderer.'

The silence hung in the air in the study for several moments, Inspector Pockett glanced uneasily at Hopkins, who was frowning to himself. Miss Frayle had eyes only for Dr. Morelle, as his gaze narrowed speculatively. A deep reverberating sigh shook Inspector Pockett's sturdy frame. 'So you're right, Dr. Morelle?' he said. 'So what do we do now?'

Dr. Morelle tapped the ash off his cigarette. 'Whoever he is, he must be feeling pretty safe now,' he said. 'He has only one person to fear, who may blow his sense of security up in his face. And at any moment.'

'Who is that?' Inspector Pockett said.

'The person who saw the murder,' Dr. Morelle said.

'You mean Brian Wickham?' Miss Frayle said.

'Brian Wickham,' Dr. Morelle said.

29

The figure waited at the wall at the back of the row of villas. The narrow, gloomy passage-way with its dustbins outside each back door was deserted. Somewhere a clock struck five-thirty, a radio dribbled dance music. The blue, sunny sky had darkened over with the threat of rain.

The figure tried the back door, but it was locked on the inside, and the shadowy form went over the wall with athletic skill, and waited in the tiny garden, listening, staring at the blank windows of the house.

The intruder moved across the garden, making for a small outhouse, whose slate roof sloped up to the window of a back bedroom which was half open. From a water-butt at the corner of the outhouse, the figure climbed on to the roof, and cat-like and silent went up towards the window.

The open lower half of the window

eased up with only a slight squeak of protest. Inside, it was still and silent. Like a wraith the intruder went over the window-sill, making no sound on the floor inside.

The still form lay in the bed, and with an intake of breath, the figure at the window darted across, and with a swift, vicious movement, whipped the pillow from underneath the sleeper's head, and pressed it down, a knee on the edge of the bed.

The sleeper struggled, legs thrashing the bedclothes, but still the pillow pressed down.

Suddenly the bedroom door crashed open, and the creature at the bed leaped up, the pillow dropping, as Dr. Morelle, Inspector Pockett and Detective-Sergeant Hopkins crowded into the little room.

With a gasp the figure moved from the bed towards the window. But Hopkins moved even more swiftly. A fist swung, there was a crunching blow as bone met bone, and the intruder staggered and fell.

It was Theodore Willard who lay flat on his back, blood ran from the corner of his mouth in a dark trickle. The detective-sergeant's blow had caught him on the side of his jaw, causing him to bite his tongue. He tried to pull himself together, but the two detectives gave him no chance, he was manhandled expertly, there was a snap of handcuffs and Inspector Pockett was saying:

'Theodore Willard, you don't want to make things tough for yourself — '

'Damn you,' Willard said, 'prove it, if you can, that I strangled the bitch.'

Inspector Pockett's gaze shifted to Dr. Morelle, who stood there, his saturnine features expressionless. 'It's my duty to warn you,' the detective said, 'that anything you say — '

There was a sound from the bed. Brian Wickham was sitting up, his face white, his hair dishevelled, blinking uncomprehendingly. He saw Theodore Willard, and cried out:

'You, it was you . . . ' He broke off, staring at the others, then he went on: 'That was who it was, Dr. Morelle.' Dr. Morelle was watching him intently. 'It's come back to me now, I saw him in

Greenacre Woods, before I fell.'

Inspector Pockett had moved forward, all his attention concentrated upon the young student. Detective-Sergeant Hopkins had one heavy hand on Willard's shoulder. Willard was slumped in a chair, his narrow head bent, staring unseeingly at the handcuffs on his wrists.

Wickham went on as if speaking to himself: 'I saw Miss Finch was going up the path. He,' with a nod at Willard, 'came out of some trees near the road and joined her.'

'Ah,' the Inspector grunted.

'I saw them struggling. I saw her go down, with his hands round her throat. They didn't see me and I ran to help her, but tripped over a root of a tree and fell, hitting my head.'

'And after that?' Dr. Morelle said quietly.

'When I came to, I was wet through. I couldn't remember anything. I must have fallen into a ditch and I crawled out, and then I walked until I met Miss Ross.'

His eyes closed, he passed a hand

across his brow and he sank back into the pillows.

There was a movement in the doorway, Mrs. Wickham stood there, anxiously, a tray in her hand. Miss Frayle stood behind her.

'Don't worry, Mrs. Wickham,' Dr. Morelle said, 'your son is all right. He will probably sleep for a little.'

Inspector Pockett gave Hopkins a nod and the two of them escorted Willard, now a shambling figure, downstairs, out of the house, and into the police car.

Dr. Morelle and Miss Frayle left Brian Wickham dozing quietly, with his mother sitting patiently at his bedside. When they got to the police station, Inspector Pockett came out to them. His face wore an expression of grim satisfaction.

'He's already started to come clean,' he said. 'It was he who did your car, all right. Seemed to have some hunch about you, Doctor. That you'd be the one who'd nail him.' He paused to give Dr. Morelle a look of admiration. Then he went on: 'The old motive. He couldn't have her so no one else should. He must have been

313

one of the few men in her life who fell for Elspeth Finch, and she just kidded him along. Dropped him flat in the end for Roy Allen. The rest of it is the way Brian Wickham told it. With the trimmings.'

A little while later Dr. Morelle had returned to the Drama Workshop with Miss Frayle, where he said good-bye to Hugo Coltman, reassuring him yet again that his career as head of his famous academy would proceed unchecked by temporary disaster.

Now he sat at the wheel of the Duesenberg, Miss Frayle smiling at him a trifle wanly. At that moment, Dr. Morelle seemed to her less a grim, avenging figure of justice, than an urbane, distinguished looking, if still somewhat remote individual who was on his way, after having spent a not uninteresting few days' visit with an old acquaintance.

Everything held a dream-like quality for Miss Frayle as Dr. Morelle switched on and the car throbbed throatily. Dr. Morelle regarded her for a moment, then he said unexpectedly: 'I don't know what plans for yourself you have formulated for the future, Miss Frayle; you may be resuming your duties here next term. If, however, you feel inclined to seek more restful employment, do look me up some time.'

Miss Frayle blinked at him. Was it an invitation to her to return to him, or not? She had a mental picture of the study at 221b, Harley Street and her heart leapt at the prospect of working there again. But was that what he meant?

Dr. Morelle smiled at her, and let in the clutch and the yellow car moved forward. 'Adieu, Miss Frayle,' he said.

'I think, Dr. Morelle,' she said. 'That is, I'd like to — '

But he did not slacken the Duesenberg's speed. 'Do telephone me some time, Miss Frayle,' he said over his shoulder. 'I shall be pleased to hear from you; and, who knows, I may be able to put a job in your way.'

And Miss Frayle watched with agitated gaze the yellow Duesenberg turn out of the drive-gates and out of sight. As the sound of the powerful engine died away on the early evening air, she was not to know that Dr. Morelle was smiling to himself in complacent anticipation as he headed back to London.

THE END

We do hope that you have enjoyed reading this large print book.

Did you know that all of our titles are available for purchase?

We publish a wide range of high quality large print books including:
Romances, Mysteries, Classics
General Fiction
Non Fiction and Westerns

Special interest titles available in large print are:
The Little Oxford Dictionary
Music Book, Song Book
Hymn Book, Service Book

Also available from us courtesy of Oxford University Press:
Young Readers' Dictionary
(large print edition)
Young Readers' Thesaurus
(large print edition)

For further information or a free brochure, please contact us at:
Ulverscroft Large Print Books Ltd.,
The Green, Bradgate Road, Anstey,
Leicester, LE7 7FU, England.
Tel: (00 44) **0116 236 4325**
Fax: (00 44) **0116 234 0205**

Other titles in the
Linford Mystery Library:

THE WHISTLING SANDS

Ernest Dudley

Along with a large cash legacy, Miss Alice Ames had inherited the Whistling Sands, an old house overlooking the Conway Estuary. And it was here she began married life with Wally Somers — alias Wally Sloane, wanted by the Sydney police. To Wally, Alice and the Whistling Sands were just a means to the money he stood to gain. But when both had come to mean more to him than that, he became enmeshed in a web of deceit — and murder . . .

PLACE MILL

Barbara Softly

In 1645, the Civil War rages and young Nicholas Lambert joins the Royalist Army, leaving his sister Katharine behind. Six years later, with the Royalists defeated, Nicholas is a fugitive. Returning home for safety, accompanied by two friends, he finds much has changed. Taking Katharine and his cousin Hester as cover, they attempt to escape to France, but encounter difficulties before even reaching the coast. And then Katharine disappears . . . Suspicious of their new acquaintances, who will they be able to trust?

DEAD WEIGHT

E. C. Tubb

Sam Falkirk, Captain in the World Police stationed at the World Council in New York, investigates the death of Angelo Augustine, a Council employee. Superficially a parcel courier, Angelo had also spied for Senator Rayburn, whose power-hungry plan is the destruction of the Orient. Meanwhile, Senator Sucamari of the Japanese legation has a deadly plan himself, involving a parcel containing a Buddha coated with enough bacteria to cause a plague across the Americas. When the parcel is stolen can Falkirk find the criminal in time?

ONE FOR THE ROAD

Peter Conway

After a car accident shatters the lives of Mike and Penny Craven, the ex-racing car driver's morale is low. However, when he sees a young woman attacked by thugs and rescues her, his life begins to take on a new meaning. But soon his courage, his skill as a driver and his marriage are all called into question as he and the young woman face violence and death at the hands of a group of vicious criminals.

TO LOVE AND PERISH

Ernest Dudley

In Castlebay, North Wales, Dick Merrill is on trial, accused of murdering his wife. Merrill, good looking and attractive, is fatally in love with Margot Stone, who is herself already married. Philip Vane, a lawyer whose career was mysteriously ruined, finds himself similarly infatuated with Margot when he becomes personally involved in Merrill's sensational murder-trial. A shadowy figure, Vane's participation in the trial is twisted and erratic — will the outcome be as unpredictable?